Jennif

Medical

BACHELOR DADS
Single Doctors…Single Fathers!

At work they are skilled medical
professionals, but at home, as soon as they
walk in the door, these eligible bachelors are
on full-time fatherhood duty!

These devoted dads still find room in their lives for love…

It takes very special women to win the hearts
of these dedicated doctors, and a very special
kind of caring to make these single fathers
full-time husbands!

Jennifer Taylor lives in the north-west of England with her husband Bill. She had been writing Mills & Boon® romances for some years, but when she discovered Medical Romances™ she was so captivated by these heart-warming stories that she set out to write them herself! When she's not writing, or doing research for her latest book, Jennifer's hobbies include reading, travel, walking her dog and retail therapy (shopping!). Jennifer claims all that bending and stretching to reach the shelves is the best exercise possible. She's always delighted to hear from readers, so do visit her at www.jennifer-taylor.com

Recent titles by the same author:

NURSE IN A MILLION
THE FOREVER ASSIGNMENT
A SPECIAL KIND OF CARING

IN HIS
LOVING CARE

BY
JENNIFER TAYLOR

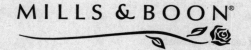

First published in Great Britain 2006
Harlequin Mills & Boon Limited,
Eton House, 18-24 Paradise Road, Richmond, Surrey TW9 1SR

© Jennifer Taylor 2006

ISBN 0 263 84721 7

Set in Times Roman 10 on 11½ pt.
03-0306-60922

Printed and bound in Spain
by Litografia Rosés, S.A., Barcelona

CHAPTER ONE

'DR COLE? I'm Helen Daniels, the senior partner. Thank you for coming.'

Helen summoned a smile as the man stood up, hoping that she didn't look as weary as she felt. The response to her advertisement for a new partner to join the staff at The Beeches surgery had been far better than she'd anticipated. Even after whittling the applications down to just a dozen, it still meant that she'd spent every spare minute this past week interviewing for the post. Lewis Cole was her final candidate and, to her mind, the most promising, although she took care not to let him know that as she escorted him from the waiting-room. She intended to choose her new partner very carefully—make the decision with her head, not her heart.

A frown puckered her brow as she led the way into her consulting-room. She had no idea why she should have imagined that she might become emotionally involved when making the decision. It had never crossed her mind while she had been interviewing the other candidates so why had it occurred to her now?

Covertly, she studied Lewis Cole as he sat down in front of her desk, taking stock of a leanly muscular physique, crisp dark brown hair and smoothly handsome features. He was wearing a beautifully tailored black suit with a white shirt and an expensive silk tie so maybe that was what had set him apart from the other candidates, she mused. None of the people she'd interviewed to date had been so formally attired and perhaps that was why he had stood out.

He suddenly looked up and Helen hastily took her seat when she found herself subjected to an equally thorough scrutiny from a pair of piercing deep grey eyes. If she'd been weighing up Lewis Cole then he was returning the favour and she couldn't help wondering what he thought of her.

Did he find her particular shade of red hair attractive, for instance? Someone had once described the colour as wet-fox red, and had meant it as a compliment, too, although the colour might not be to everyone's taste. The warm greeny-blue colour of her eyes wasn't too bad, though, and her features were even enough...

'Thank you for seeing me, Dr Daniels. I know my application was a little late reaching you but I didn't notice your advertisement when I first read the journal.'

Helen jumped when Lewis Cole addressed her in a voice that sounded like dark chocolate—all smooth and rich and velvety. She quickly returned her attention to what she was supposed to be doing, rather surprised that it had wavered in the first place. Taking his application out of her tray, she placed it in the centre of her blotter.

'I did request that the advertisement should be placed inside a box so it would stand out, but my instructions weren't carried out.' She treated him to a cool smile, wanting to regain control of the interview and not allow him to hijack it, as she sensed he might do. 'Fortunately, it didn't cause too many problems at the end of the day. I received over fifty applications for the post, which is an excellent result.'

'Indeed it is.'

He leant back in his chair, crossing one long leg over the other as though he was totally at ease, and Helen felt another ripple run through her. In light of the experience she'd gained during the past week, it seemed incredible that a candidate should be this relaxed during an interview so what made Dr Cole so sure of himself?

She cast another glance at his application, facts leaping out at her from the expertly typed pages: aged forty; member of the Royal College of Surgeons as well as the Royal College of Physicians; senior consultant in gastrointestinal surgery at St Leona's in London; retrained as a GP the previous year…

She looked up, wondering not for the first time why he'd decided to quit surgery. He'd stated in his application that it had been "for personal reasons", although she had no idea what that meant. Maybe it was time she found out.

'There is no point me asking you the usual questions I've asked a lot of the other candidates, Dr Cole.' She glanced at his application and shrugged. 'It's obvious from this that you have a great deal of experience so what interests me most is why you decided to leave surgery and retrain at this stage in your career.'

'As I explained in my application, my reasons were personal ones. Surgery is a very demanding discipline and it involves long and very irregular hours. At the present time I need a job that will provide me with a little more stability in my life.'

His grey eyes met hers calmly across the desk but she could see a nerve ticking in his jaw and realised with a jolt that his composure wasn't as solid as she'd imagined it to be. For some reason the discovery made her want to reassure him that he had nothing to worry about, only there was no way she could do that.

Helen sat up straighter, annoyed with herself for ignoring her own sage advice about not letting herself become emotionally involved. Lewis Cole was just another candidate and she mustn't allow herself to be swayed by the thought that she might be able to make his life a little easier by offering him the job.

'So you believe that general practice is an easier option than surgery?' she asked, allowing a hint of scepticism to creep into her voice.

'Not easier, no. Just more…predictable.'

'Predictable?' Helen tipped back her head and laughed. It was the funniest answer she'd heard all week.

'Obviously, I've said something to amuse you, Dr Daniels.'

The deep voice was colder now, stern, too, and her laughter immediately dried up. 'I laughed more in astonishment than amusement, actually. General practice is never predictable, as you'll find out for yourself if you secure a position as a GP.'

She allowed that to sink in, feeling a bit mean about slipping the doubt into the conversation, although maybe she was doing him a favour. After all, there was no guarantee that he would get this job, or any other for that matter.

The thought of his potential disappointment was upsetting for some reason and she hurried on. 'You never know what's going to happen from one minute to the next. Every time a patient walks through the door, you have to be prepared to deal with whatever they throw at you.'

She glanced at his application again then looked up, expecting to see some sign of emotion on his face, but his expression was completely blank now, as though he was deliberately hiding his feelings from her.

It was unsettling to wonder what was going on inside his head but Helen refused to dwell on it as she continued in the same no-nonsense tone. 'It's not all colds and heartburn in general practice. We have many patients at The Beeches who have very complex needs and we make sure they all receive the highest standard of care.'

'It's good to know that,' he said quietly. 'And I apologise if you thought I was being flippant. I'm certainly not dismissive of general practice work otherwise I wouldn't have chosen to become a GP myself.'

There was no doubting his sincerity. Helen felt a little heat run through her veins as she realised that she probably deserved the rebuke. She experienced a sudden urge to apologise to him before it struck her that the whole reason for this interview was so she could ask him questions like that. She took a quick breath, determined not to let herself get side-tracked again.

'The Beeches is a very busy practice. We have over three thousand patients on our books and we cover a large area of the surrounding countryside as well as the town. Whoever is appointed to this post will be a highly visible member of the local community.'

'I don't have a problem with that.' He shrugged, his broad shoulders moving lightly under the expensively tailored jacket. 'It will make a refreshing change after living in London all my adult life, in fact.'

'Good,' she said firmly, pleased to have got back onto familiar territory. So long as she stuck to the demands of the job, there wouldn't be a problem with this interview. 'Ian was very keen to ensure that The Beeches would continue to be at the heart of any local activities.'

'Ian?' he interjected.

'My husband.' Helen paused, wondering why she felt so uncomfortable about explaining her marital status. It wasn't as though she hadn't had enough time to get over Ian's death but she felt...*odd* about having to explain to Lewis Cole that she was a widow. However, there really was no way that she could avoid it.

'Ian died two years ago of a heart attack. It was a shock because he'd always been extremely fit.' She hurried on, knowing it would be easier to tell him all the details in one fell swoop. 'I took over the practice after his death and I've tried to carry on running it in a way that Ian and his father would have approved of. Ian's father founded The Beeches,' she added. 'Summerfield didn't have a doctor's surgery until then.'

'It must be very difficult for you.'

Helen felt her heart squeeze in an extra beat when she glimpsed a hint of compassion in his eyes. It made her feel very strange to know that he sympathised with her, although she couldn't allow it to affect her judgement. 'Being a widow doesn't affect my work,' she said sharply.

'I wasn't referring to that. I meant that it must be difficult to maintain someone else's standards. Most people prefer to do things their own way, in my experience.'

She blinked in surprise. Although she would never have admitted it, sometimes she did grow weary of the continual demands that were placed upon her. Living up to Ian's expectations these last two years hadn't been easy. Several times she'd been tempted to adopt a simpler approach but she'd always held back because she hadn't wanted to overrule her late husband's wishes. To have that very fact pointed out to her by this *stranger* made a lump come to her throat all of a sudden.

'I'm sorry. It wasn't my place to make such an observation.'

She wasn't sure if Lewis Cole had noticed her emotionally charged state and didn't stop to wonder about it. She couldn't afford to get embroiled in that kind of pointless exercise. She picked up his application again, hoping he would have the sensitivity not to pursue the subject.

'I see that you studied medicine at Oxford.'

'That's right. After that I did a stint at Guy's—the usual house officer nightmare of being shunted around from pillar to post— before I opted for surgery.'

'What made you decide to specialise in gastrointestinal surgery?' she asked, slipping in the question as soon as he'd finished speaking because it seemed wiser to fill all the time that she'd allotted for this interview with questions.

She shot a surreptitious glance at the clock and sighed in relief when she saw that ten minutes had passed. After another ten minutes she would be able to wind up the interview without appearing too hasty. She should be able to manage ten more minutes of Lewis Cole's company....

Or ten more years, an insidious little voice whispered inside her head. Couldn't she just imagine them working side by side in the surgery for years to come? Or, better still, spending time together outside work?

Appalled by the way her mind seemed to be behaving that

day, Helen rushed on before he'd had a chance to answer her question. 'It's one of the less glamorous specialities, isn't it?'

'I didn't go into surgery for the glamour of the job.' His tone was flat but she could sense him bridling and inwardly groaned because now she would have to apologise.

'I'm sure you didn't. It was an unfortunate choice of words,' she said as calmly as she could, unsure why she was so wary. After all, a simple apology shouldn't have been a major issue, yet for some reason she felt uneasy about letting him gain the upper hand.

He inclined his head so she took it to mean that he'd accepted her attempt to make amends. However, it seemed wiser not to say anything else in case any more unruly thoughts came rushing out of her mouth. She waited politely for him to continue and after a moment he carried on.

'I chose gastrointestinal surgery for the simple reason that not many surgeons choose to work in that particular field.'

'I see,' Helen replied automatically, although she didn't really understand. Maybe it showed, too, because he explained without her having to prompt him.

'I was extremely ambitious when I began my career in medicine. I intended to make consultant by the time I was thirty-five and I achieved my aim. I might not have succeeded if I'd gone into a different speciality like orthopaedics, for instance. That's always a popular choice for budding surgeons.'

'So your interest in gastrointestinal surgery was a career choice?' she clarified, somewhat surprised by his honesty.

'Partly, yes. Obviously I had an interest in the field otherwise I would never have opted for it. However, my main reason for choosing it was to achieve personal progression.'

'Yet you've chosen to retrain as a general practitioner? Don't you find it somewhat daunting to be back on the bottom rung of the career ladder?' she asked bluntly, needing to understand his motivation better.

She'd obviously surprised him by the forthright question because that nerve in his jaw had started to beat even faster now. Nevertheless, his gaze was level as he looked at her across the desk.

'Yes, I do. I find it extremely daunting. However, it's what I need to do so that's all there is to it.'

He glanced down and when he looked up again she could see the conviction in his eyes. 'Maybe my route to becoming a GP has been a little unorthodox but I promise you, Dr Daniels, that if you do take me on as a partner I will do the job to the very best of my ability. There will be no half-measures, I assure you. I will give you one hundred per cent commitment.'

Lewis tried to hide his anxiety beneath an outward aura of calm but his blood pressure was going through the roof! However, if he'd learned one thing during the past twelve months it was that he desperately needed to put some stability into his and Kristy's lives, and moving to Summerfield could be the perfect way to do it.

His mouth twisted wryly because there was very little about this situation that could be classed as perfect. A year ago his life had been structured almost to a fault but now he never knew from one day to the next what was going to happen. Looking after a six-year-old child, and a child who had suffered several major traumas in her short life, was far more challenging than anything he'd done before, but his determination had never wavered. Kristy deserved the happiness and security that came from knowing she was loved.

The sheer force of his feelings whenever he thought about his daughter was in danger of making his composure crumble so he did his best to batten down his emotions. Helen Daniels was staring at his application as though it was the most fascinating thing she'd ever read but he sensed that her concentration was a cover for less positive thoughts.

Couldn't she imagine herself working with him? he wondered anxiously because he had no idea what he was going to do if he didn't get this job.

He'd been for six interviews to date and each time another candidate had been offered the position. He knew it wasn't his lack of experience in general practice work that had been his downfall—the other candidates had been younger than him and newly qualified, too. His trouble was that he came across as far too forceful during an interview, but it was difficult to curb his natural tendency to take charge. He'd had a team of surgeons answering to him at St Leona's, although he hadn't made any mention of that in his application in case it had gone against him. He needed this job and he couldn't afford to lose it because he scared off the lovely Dr Daniels!

A frown drew Lewis's brows together. He hadn't realised until that moment that he'd noticed how attractive Helen Daniels was. With that glorious red hair and those expressive greeny-blue eyes, she was a truly beautiful woman. The fact that her expression held an innate sweetness was another plus factor because in his rather extensive experience beauty rarely equated with a charming nature. However, it appeared that Helen Daniels had been blessed with both and it was unnerving to realise that he was attracted to her. The last thing he could afford was to find himself embroiled in a relationship when he had Kristy to consider.

'I don't doubt that you mean what you say, Dr Cole. However, I would be lying if I said that I don't have reservations about offering you the job.'

Helen Daniel's voice cut through his thoughts like a hot knife through butter, and he stiffened. He stared back at her, blanking out every thought apart from the fact that he had to get this job.

'Because of my lack of experience in general practice work?' he suggested neutrally, and she shrugged.

'That's not my main concern. I'm sure you would cope admirably in whichever field you chose to work. However, working in a town like Summerfield would be a whole new experience for most people, and it would be vastly different to what you're used to.'

'In what way?' he demanded, struggling to remain calm, no easy feat when he knew where the conversation was leading. Helen Daniels was trying to let him down as gently as possible but he didn't want to be let down—didn't want to let *Kristy* down when she was depending on him!

'There is nothing hi-tech about this practice. We've always relied on the principle of good, accurate diagnosis followed by the appropriate treatment. After-care is also extremely important to us so we make sure that we don't lose touch with our patients once we've treated them.'

'I agree.' Lewis summoned a smile, hoping it would disguise his chagrin. Dr Daniels obviously didn't rate him very highly if she thought that she needed to explain that principle to him.

'It's an approach I employed at St Leona's. Every patient I treated there was called back for a further consultation six weeks after their surgery and I made a point of seeing them myself rather than relying on a junior to do it for me. Not only did it enable me to assess their fitness, it also gave me the opportunity to fine-tune the treatment I'd provided for them and maybe improve on it for the next patient I saw.'

'Oh! I hadn't realised that.'

Lewis felt a wave of tenderness wash over him when he saw a little colour touch her cheeks. His tone softened, taking on a gentleness that he rarely employed apart from when he was speaking to Kristy.

'There's no reason why you should have known, Dr Daniels. The work I did at St Leona's was vastly different to what you do here. I understand that. I'm also aware that I still have a great deal to learn about general practice work. However, I've completed my training and the experience I gained during that time has given me an insight into what might be expected of me.'

'Of course,' she replied stiffly, obviously embarrassed by her gaffe. 'I never meant to imply otherwise, Dr Cole, I assure you.'

'I'm sure you didn't,' he replied smoothly. He certainly didn't want to make her feel that she was in the wrong when it could have repercussions on her offering him the job. He needed this job for Kristy's sake and wanted it for himself, too. He could imagine himself working very happily with Helen Daniels.

Lewis cleared his throat, somewhat surprised by the thought. It was rare for him to make snap judgements and he couldn't understand why he'd done so in this instance. 'All I can say is that I will do a good job if you offer me the post. With your help, I feel that I could fit in here and make a valuable contribution to the community.'

'I appreciate your enthusiasm, Dr Cole. However, as I'm sure you will understand, I need to consider your application in light of the others I've received. The standard has been extremely high so it may take a few days for me to reach a decision.'

She stood up, making it clear that the interview was over. Lewis's heart sank as he got to his feet. He knew without having to be told that he'd blown it. He'd been too forceful, too sure of himself, and she wasn't having any of it.

He really couldn't blame her, he thought as he shook her hand. He would have had reservations, too, if he'd been the one doing the interview. A forty-year-old consultant surgeon moving into general practice wasn't the usual run-of-the-mill candidate so any prospective employer would have had doubts. Not for the first time he found himself wondering if he'd been mad to take this step, yet what choice had he had?

Kristy needed him to be there when she got home from school. She needed him to be there in the middle of the night when she woke up, screaming in terror. What use was he to her if he was stuck in Theatre or at one of the endless fundraising dinners he'd been expected to attend? His whole lifestyle had had to change, although he didn't regret it for a second. He owed Kristy this and a lot more after the way he'd failed her for the first six years of her life!

He swung round, wishing there was something more he could have done to convince Helen Daniels that he was the best candidate for the post. She followed him from the room and he could sense her eagerness to get rid of him as she escorted him to the reception area. She paused by the desk, a polite smile fixed to her lovely mouth, and he sighed. There was no point holding out any hope that he would be offered the job so maybe he should cut his losses and make this as easy as possible for her.

'Thank you for seeing me, Dr Daniels. I appreciate you giving up your time.'

'Thank you for coming all this way,' she countered politely. 'Did you drive up here or travel by train, by the way?'

'I drove. The trains can be a little erratic and I wanted to make sure I was back when Kristy got home from school,' he replied, without thinking, because he was busily watching the light from the window playing across her hair. It really was the most glorious colour, he thought, watching a winter sunbeam bounce fiery lights off the silky red tendrils…

'You have a daughter?'

The surprise in her voice reclaimed his attention and he nodded. 'Yes. Kristy is six,' he explained in the noncommittal tone he used whenever anyone exhibited surprise at the fact that he was a father.

'A lovely age. Old enough to enjoy her company yet still young enough that you can take care of her. You spend all your time worrying about them when they're old enough to leave home.'

Lewis frowned. He wasn't sure what to make of that comment. He would have put her age at somewhere in her mid-thirties so she must have been very young when she'd had her family if her children had left home. Bearing in mind the years she would have spent studying, it seemed very strange and he was still trying to work it out when she continued.

'How does your wife feel about moving out of London? Is she happy about the idea?'

Lewis forgot about Helen's family as he tried to decide how to answer the question. Normally, he avoided any mention of Tessa because he found it too difficult to talk about her. It also upset Kristy to hear her mother's name mentioned so he skirted around the subject whenever anyone asked about her. However, for some reason he felt that he had to be truthful with Helen Daniels.

'I'm not married. I never have been, in fact.'

'Oh! I'm sorry. I just assumed you were when you spoke about your daughter…'

She broke off in embarrassment and he grimaced because now he'd made matters worse. The only way to rectify the problem was to tell her the full story and to hell with what she thought…only it wasn't that simple. For some, inexplicable reason he didn't want her to think badly of him.

'Kristy's mother and I had a brief affair some years ago before she moved to Florida. She never told me that she was pregnant before she left so I had no idea that she was expecting my child. I only found out last year when a firm of lawyers from Miami informed me that I had a daughter.'

'It must have been a shock for you.'

'It was.' He smiled grimly, thinking that must be the biggest understatement of all time. Even now, a full year later, he still woke up at night sometimes and wondered if he'd dreamt it.

'You said that you found out about your daughter when you were contacted by lawyers? Was there a reason for that?'

Lewis felt his heart swell when he saw the concern in her beautiful eyes. It had been a long time since anyone had looked at him that way, he thought wistfully. He realised that he needed to terminate the conversation before he got in way too deep for his own good. Once he left The Beeches that would be the last he saw of Helen Daniels so there was no point wallowing in all that wonderful sympathy.

'Unfortunately, Tessa was involved in a road accident and subsequently died of her injuries. She was living with some guy in Miami at the time, and after she died he decided that he didn't want to be responsible for Kristy.' He shrugged, trying to damp down the anger he felt whenever he thought about what had happened. 'He took off one day and left Kristy in the apartment. Fortunately, a neighbour heard her crying and called the police, but from what they could gather she'd been on her own for almost a week by then.'

'But that's awful!' Helen exclaimed. 'How could anyone just abandon a young child?'

'I've no idea. Anyway, once the authorities discovered that Tessa was dead, they put Kristy into care. It was only when the police finally tracked down the guy Tessa had been living with that my name cropped up. Tessa had told him I was Kristy's father, so the lawyer who was working on the case got in touch with me. I flew out to Miami the following day and was granted custody of her.'

'It must have been a huge shock for you, though.'

'It was.' He smiled wryly. 'I'd never thought about having a family and all of a sudden I had a six-year-old daughter I had never even known existed.'

'You could have had her adopted,' she said, her eyes locked to his face in a way that would have bothered him if it hadn't been for what she'd said. The fact that she believed him capable of giving up his own child made him see just how low an opinion she had of him, and it hurt to realise that, hurt far more than it should have done, bearing in mind that he barely knew her.

'Kristy is my child and I would never put her up for adoption,' he stated in a voice like steel. 'I've enough to feel guilty about without adding that into the equation.'

'But you didn't even know that you had a daughter!' she protested.

'No, I didn't know about her, but that isn't an excuse for what's gone on. The poor child has suffered enough heartache in her young life and I intend to do everything I can to make up for it.'

He looked straight into her eyes, wanting to convince her yet unsure why it mattered so much. 'I'm going to do my best to be the perfect father to her, and if that means giving up my career and moving home then that's what I shall do. The only person who matters now is Kristy and there is nothing I won't do to make her happy!'

CHAPTER TWO

'THERE'S a staff meeting today at twelve. It will be a bit of rush to fit it in before we do the house calls but we find it helpful to get together a couple of times a week to discuss any problems we have.'

Helen summoned a smile, wishing she didn't feel so on edge whenever she had to speak to Lewis. After all, it had been her decision to offer him the job so it wasn't as though she hadn't had any choice in the matter. Would she have taken him on if he hadn't told her about his daughter, though? she wondered all of a sudden.

She'd already decided that she wasn't going to offer him the job when he'd told her about Kristy, and it had been that which had made her reconsider. The thought of what the child had been through had had a huge bearing on her decision, although it hadn't been the only reason she'd changed her mind. It had been Lewis's determination to do all he could for the little girl which had been the deciding factor, and it was unsettling to know that he had that much power over her. It wasn't surprising that she felt so nervous around him in the circumstances.

'Fine by me. There's a couple of queries I'd like to raise.'

He smiled ruefully and Helen's heart performed the strangest manoeuvre—something between a leap and a hiccup. She had to make a determined effort to concentrate as he continued in the same wry tone.

'My lack of experience in some areas of general practice work is starting to show so I'm hoping the rest of the team can give me a few pointers.'

'That's what we're here for,' she agreed briskly, deciding that enough was enough. She made her way to the door, pausing reluctantly when he spoke again. She would have preferred to make her escape rather than risk a few more seconds in his company.

'I forgot to ask whose car we're going in this afternoon to do the home visits. I don't mind driving if you feel like a break.'

'We'll go in mine,' she said shortly. It was irritating to have these ideas flashing into her head all the time. She'd worked with Ian for over twelve years and not once had she experienced even a hint of the awareness around him which she felt around Lewis.

The thought was less comforting that it should have been and she hurried on. 'We need to visit one of the local farms today and your car really isn't suitable.'

'Hmm. A sports car isn't the ideal vehicle to get around the area, is it?'

He sighed as he tossed his pen onto the desk and stretched his arms above his head. Helen looked away when muscles began to ripple beneath his shirt. She was trying to defuse the tension, not add to it!

'I'm going to have to bite the bullet and change my car, I suppose.' He heaved another sigh then dropped his hands onto the desk in a gesture that smacked of defeat.

'Obviously a major sacrifice,' she said tartly, because it seemed safer not to sympathise with him as she would have done with any other member of the staff.

'Oh, I'm not worried for myself. A car is a car, so far as I'm concerned, but Kristy loves it. The only time I've heard her laugh, in fact, was when I took her to the seaside in the summer and we put the top down. I think it reminded her of drives with her mother. Tessa was driving a convertible when she was killed.'

Helen immediately felt guilty. It had been wrong of her to try and offset the effect he had on her by thinking badly of him.

'How is Kristy settling in?' she asked, because there was no way that she could apologise for being so sharp with him. It would only make him wonder why she'd spoken to him in that fashion in the first place, and that was the last thing she needed.

'So far, so good.' He crossed his fingers. 'She seems to like her new school well enough and the fact that there's an after-school club has been a real bonus. I've not had to find a child-minder to look after her until I get home from work. However, what really swung it was the house. The place we're renting backs onto a farm and there's a horse in the paddock. Kristy spends all her spare time standing by the fence, stroking it!'

Helen laughed. 'A lot of little girls are mad about horses. I know I was at her age. Maybe you should think about booking some riding lessons for her.'

'Actually, I have it on my list of things to do. Unfortunately, it's a very long list and I haven't got round to it yet.' He tipped back his chair and smiled at her. Helen's heart performed another interesting manoeuvre, a kind of double somersault this time.

'I can imagine,' she said as calmly as she could. 'It must be difficult to keep on top of everything with moving house and starting a new job.'

'Tell me about it! There don't seem to be enough hours in a day to fit everything in. But arranging for Kristy to have riding lessons should be a priority, really. I don't suppose you know where the nearest stables are?'

'I'm afraid there aren't any in Summerfield.'

'That's a blow. I was hoping I'd be able to find somewhere local to take her for lessons.'

'Jill Sandford at Sandy Brook farm is a qualified instructor. She used to take a few pupils so maybe you could try phoning her?' she suggested, hating to hear him sounding so deflated.

'That's a great idea! Can you let me have her number? I'll give her a call tonight after work.'

'I'll hunt it out for you. And now I really must get down to some work.'

She quickly excused herself and made her way to her room. There were three consulting rooms at The Beeches, plus a treatment room which was normally occupied by Amy, their practice nurse. Helen had taken over Ian's room after he'd died because it was the sunniest, while Harry Scott, their locum, was currently using the room she'd once had. She'd given Lewis the room that had belonged to Ian's father and now she found herself wishing that she'd arranged to have it decorated. It had always been a gloomy room and a fresh lick of paint would have brightened it up. She should have got rid of some of the old-fashioned furniture, too. Ian had insisted on keeping the room exactly as his father had left it, but it was time the place was updated.

She frowned as she opened the door to her own room. It, too, desperately needed modernising. Ian had always refused to modernise the surgery but maybe it was time she did so. She couldn't keep clinging to the past because it was what Ian would have wanted. She had to make her own decisions and it was a surprise to find herself thinking along such lines. She wasn't sure what had sparked it off so she tried to forget about it as she summoned her first patient. There would be time enough for colour charts and fabric swatches later!

Her first patient was Diane Hartley, a teacher at the local high school. Helen smiled when she came into the room. 'Hello, Diane. It's not often I see you here on a weekday.'

'No, and I feel dreadful about taking time off work, too, but I just had to come and see you.'

She suddenly burst into tears so Helen quickly got up and led her to the chair next to her desk. 'Here, take this,' she said, handing Diane a tissue. She waited while the other woman wiped her eyes then smiled at her. 'Now, tell me what's wrong.'

'I don't know! That's the trouble. I feel so miserable all the time and I can't seem to stop crying.' Diane blew her nose. 'It's as though there's this black cloud hanging over me all the time. It's driving poor Martin mad.'

'I'm sure Martin is more concerned about you than anything else,' Helen assured her. She certainly didn't want to add to the poor woman's woes by encouraging her to worry about how her husband was feeling. 'When did this all start?'

'It's been going on for a while now,' Diane admitted. 'I just kept telling myself to stop being so silly but it's got to the point now where I don't know what to do. I can't keep on feeling this awful all the time, Dr Daniels. Life isn't worth living.'

'Then we need to do something about it,' Helen said firmly, standing up. 'I'm going to examine you to get an idea of how your health is generally and we'll take it from there.'

She examined Diane and found nothing to alarm her. Putting her stethoscope away, she went to one of the cupboards. 'I'd like to take a blood sample, if you wouldn't mind. We need to find out if there's a physical cause for the way you're feeling.'

'Of course I don't mind!' Diane sounded so relieved that Helen looked at her in surprise. Diane blushed. 'I thought I was having some sort of mental breakdown. There's a lot of pressure in my job and I assumed it was that which was causing the problem.'

'It could very well be a factor,' Helen agreed. 'However, these feelings you've been experiencing could also be the result of physical changes in your body. Have you noticed anything else unusual happening recently?'

'Well, yes, now that you mention it, I've been having these terrible hot spells. I wake up at night because I'm dripping wet. And my periods have become very irregular, too. I've always been like clockwork but I never know when I'm going to come on nowadays. Do you think they might be linked to how miserable I've been feeling lately?'

Helen chose her words with care. There could be a common factor linking all those symptoms and one that Diane might not be happy about, either. 'It's possible, if your oestrogen levels have dropped.'

'My oestrogen levels…' Diane repeated, then gasped. 'You don't think I could be going through the menopause, do you? I mean, I'm only thirty-six so surely it's far too early for that to happen?'

'I don't intend to make any snap judgements today. However, you told me last year that you and Martin were trying for a baby so it's possible that you haven't conceived because your fertility levels have fallen. The blood test will confirm that, one way or the other.'

'But does that mean I won't be able to have a baby now?' Diane asked in dismay.

'I really can't say what will happen until I know exactly what's going on, Diane,' Helen replied gently, uncapping a syringe and taking an alcohol swab out of its foil packet.

'How long will it take to find out?' Diane demanded, wincing as the needle slid into her arm.

'Just a couple of days.' Helen carefully withdrew the small amount of blood she needed for the tests and smiled reassuringly. 'I'll give it top priority so we should have the results back by the end of the week. And I'll phone you immediately once I get them.'

'And if it is the onset of the menopause, then what happens? Is there anything you can do to stop it?'

'If it is that, I shall refer you to a fertility specialist. There's a very good clinic near Blackpool which has achieved some excellent results. But it's all speculation at this stage. We need to see those results before we know what we're dealing with.'

Diane sighed as she stood up. 'I don't know what I'm hoping for now. If the tests show that I'm going through an early menopause, it will explain why I've been feeling so dreadful, but it could also mean that Martin and I might never have a family.'

'I know how difficult it must be for you but at least we're doing something positive and that's the main thing.'

Helen made herself sound as upbeat as possible as she saw Diane out. However, she couldn't helping drawing a comparison with her own situation. She was thirty-eight and her own fertility levels must be dropping, too. Ian had never wanted them to have a child because he'd had the twins. His first wife had died

soon after Helen had started her GP training at The Beeches and
it had seemed the most natural thing in the world to offer her help
when Ian had found it difficult to manage with two small children to look after on top of doing his job.

Tom and Katie had been six when she had married Ian, and
by that time she had loved them as much as she would have loved
her own children. However, she couldn't deny that it had been
a blow when she'd found out that Ian hadn't wanted to add to
their family. She'd kept hoping that he would change his mind,
but it hadn't happened. Now it seemed unlikely that she would
ever give birth to her own son or daughter, and she couldn't help
feeling sad at the thought of what she was missing.

No wonder Lewis was so determined to do all he could for
his daughter, she thought, then sighed in exasperation. Why did
every single thought lead back to Lewis?

Lewis was late for the meeting, mainly because he still hadn't
got used to judging the length of time he could spend with each
patient. Six minutes were allotted for each consultation and it
was far too little in his opinion. Harry and Amy were already sitting at the staffroom table with an open tin of biscuits in front
of them when he arrived. Helen was pouring coffee and she
glanced round when he appeared.

'Black or white?'

'Black, please, with plenty of sugar.'

'Sounds like you had a hard morning,' Amy said, grinning as
he sat down. A pretty girl in her twenties, she was engaged to a
policeman and in the throes of planning a summer wedding.

'I haven't adjusted to the conveyor-belt system you operate
here so I find it difficult to keep up.' He rolled his eyes.
'Switching my brain from what analgesic to prescribe for a
teething toddler to how to treat Mr Parsons's gout all in the
space of a couple of minutes takes some doing!'

'It must be your age,' Amy retorted. 'That's why you can't
keep up.'

'Cheeky monkey!' Lewis laughed out loud. It was refreshing to be treated as just another member of the team after the awe he'd inspired in his previous post. 'I'll remind you of that in a few years' time when you're having problems keeping up the pace.'

'Ah, but I'll still be younger than you so I'll still fare better,' Amy countered.

'Touché!' He shook his head in defeat because he obviously wasn't going to win this argument. He glanced round when Helen brought over the coffee, feeling his heart leap when her hand accidentally brushed against his as she placed it in front of him.

'Thanks.' Picking up the mug, he took a gulp of the coffee in the hope that it would steady him, but his hand was still tingling from the contact and it worried him that he should be so aware of her. He'd had his share of relationships and didn't intend to have any more until Kristy was all grown up and no longer needed him. And by that time he'd be too old to bother!

'Is Mr Parsons's gout getting worse?'

Helen sat down opposite him and he hastily returned his thoughts to the reason for the meeting. He was supposed to be discussing his patients' problems, not thinking about his own.

'It's spread to his ankle now and he's in a lot of pain. The joint is very red and swollen, and obviously tender. Unfortunately, he forgot to renew his prescription after the last bout so he didn't have any medication to stave it off. I gave him an injection of corticosteroids and another script. I also took some blood to check his levels of uric acid. He might need a new drug and diet regime to reduce the levels of uric acid in his body and help his kidneys excrete it more quickly. I noticed from his file that it's two years since his last review so he must be due for one.'

'He is. Let me know when the test results come back and we can discuss it then.' She put her mug down and reached for the biscuit tin at the same moment as he went to get it. Once again their hands touched and he jerked his back when he felt the current of electricity that arced between them.

'Of course, if you're interested,' he replied thickly, struggling to get a grip on himself.

'Tom Parsons is one of our oldest patients. He was the first person to sign on when the practice opened so naturally I'm interested,' Helen replied neutrally, so neutrally, in fact, that he couldn't help wondering if she'd felt the electricity, too.

He shot her a wary glance but it was impossible to tell what she was thinking, and maybe it was better that he couldn't. There was no room in his life for Helen or any other woman when he had Kristy to consider. The thought steadied him and he looked calmly at her. 'I can't imagine having patients for that length of time. Most of the people I treated at St Leona's I saw just a couple of times—once before their surgery and once after it was over.'

'It's totally different here,' Harry put in, helping himself to a biscuit. 'Most of the folk we see have been on our books for years. Talk about from the cradle to the grave isn't in it!'

Lewis smiled at the wry note in the younger man's voice. 'Don't you approve?'

'Oh, it's great if you like that sort of thing.' Harry grimaced. 'It's just not for me. I want a bit of excitement in my life before I settle for the old pipe and slippers routine. To be honest, I can't imagine why you decided to swop an interesting job in London for working here…no offence intended, Helen,' he added as an obvious afterthought.

'And none taken,' she replied smoothly. 'I know this is just a stopgap for you, Harry, before you move on to bigger and better things.'

'I didn't mean it that way,' the younger man said uncomfortably. 'I enjoy working here but I wouldn't want to spend the rest of my days doing the same job. The Beeches is great the way it looks after all its patients so wonderfully, but it's a bit of a throwback to another era. Very few general practices offer the kind of all-encompassing service we provide.'

'Maybe they don't but The Beeches was founded on the principle of commitment and caring, and that's something I'm proud of and intend to continue,' Helen said firmly. She turned and Lewis stiffened when he saw the challenge in her eyes. 'How do you feel, Lewis? Do you think we're out of date in the way we do things here?'

'I think you could cut out a lot of the unnecessary work,' he said carefully, not wanting to offend her.

'Really? Would you care to elaborate?'

She stared back at him and he sighed when he saw the glint in her beautiful eyes. He really and truly didn't want to start an argument but, now that she'd asked for his opinion, he felt duty bound to give it.

'A lot of patients we see don't actually need to be seen by a doctor. They could visit the local pharmacy and buy something over the counter for their cough or their cold. If we could be more selective when making appointments then we could spend extra time on the people who really do need our help.'

'And how do you propose we sort out who does and who doesn't need an appointment?' she shot back.

He shrugged. 'Most general practices use their reception staff to separate the wheat from the chaff, so to speak.'

'I'm sure they do. However, the reception staff aren't medically qualified so how can they assess if a patient really needs to see one of us? If we ask them to make decisions like that, there is the risk of someone who is really sick not getting an appointment.'

'That's a valid point. However, the reception staff could be trained to ask a few simple questions when people phone for an appointment,' he pointed out, although he suspected there was little hope of persuading her to adopt a different policy. However, it seemed wrong to him that their lists should be cluttered up with people who really didn't need to see a doctor when it put added pressure on everyone.

Helen, for instance, could spare herself a lot of work if she would make a few simple changes to the way the practice was run. In the week he'd been there, he'd discovered that she was the first to arrive each morning and the last to leave each night. She didn't even take an afternoon off like the rest of them did. She worked far too hard and it seemed wrong to him that she felt that she had to devote her every waking minute to the job.

'I'm afraid I wouldn't be at all happy with that idea.' She pushed back her chair, making it clear that she didn't intend to discuss the matter further. However, now that he'd got this far, Lewis wasn't prepared to let it drop without a fight.

'If it's change that worries you then it's always the first step that's the most difficult.' He shrugged when she looked sharply at him. 'It gets easier after that.'

'Thank you for that sage advice, Dr Cole. However, I'm the senior partner in this practice and I shall decide how best to run it.'

'But Lewis has made a legitimate point,' Harry interjected. 'Take this morning, for instance. I saw three people who had colds and nothing else wrong with them. It's a waste of our time to have to deal with things like that when folk would be better off at home in bed.'

'Thank you for your contribution, Harry, but I think I've made my feelings on the matter perfectly clear. The Beeches has been run on an open-house basis ever since it was opened and I can see no reason to change the system at this point in time.'

She marched to the door, pausing to shoot an icy look over her shoulder. Lewis winced when he received the full brunt of her displeasure. 'I'll see you in the car park in ten minutes' time. We have a full list of calls to get through so I'd appreciate it if you didn't keep me waiting.'

With that she swept out of the door, leaving behind her a small but potent silence, broken when Harry cleared his throat.

'Ahem! That went down rather well, don't you think?'

'Like a lead balloon.' Lewis downed the rest of his coffee then got up to leave, knowing it would be unwise to keep Helen waiting. It had been her idea to accompany him to any home visits during his first week. She'd offered to introduce him to the patients and make sure that he knew where he was going. However, he couldn't help wishing that she'd left him to his own devices. The thought of spending an afternoon with her after what had happened was less than appealing.

'I still think you were right to say what you did.' Harry gathered up their cups and took them to the sink. 'Don't you, Amy?'

'I do. We need to cut down the amount of work we do otherwise we're going to sink under the sheer number of patients we're expected to see each day. I was hoping things might improve when Helen took over, but she's not changed a thing. She runs this place along exactly the same lines as Ian and his father always did.'

'Why is she so reluctant to alter the routine?' Lewis asked curiously.

'I'm not sure.' Amy shrugged. 'Maybe it's her way of keeping Ian's memory alive. If she changes things then it might seem that she's trying to get rid of everything he held dear. But something needs to be done otherwise she's going to run herself into the ground. Since the twins took off for Australia on their gap year trip before university, Helen has been working harder than ever. I think she's lonely, although she'd never admit it.'

'Her children are old enough to go to university?' he exclaimed in amazement.

'Oh, they're not actually her kids, not biologically anyway,' Amy explained hurriedly. 'Ian was married before and when his wife died, Helen helped him look after the twins. They were only toddlers at the time and a real handful from what my mum has told me. She used to be the practice nurse before she retired and she was here when it happened. Helen was doing her GP training at the time but she stayed on after Ian's first wife died and married Ian a couple of years later.'

'I see. So does Helen have any children of her own, as well as the twins, I mean?' he asked, wanting to form a clearer picture of the situation because it seemed important for some reason.

'No. From what Mum has said, I don't think Ian wanted any more children so he and Helen never had any.' Amy sighed. 'I think it was a bit mean of him, actually. I get the impression that she would have loved a baby of her own. She's wonderful with the little ones—they all adore her.'

Very mean indeed, he thought grimly as he left the staffroom, although he took care not to say so. Helen's reluctance to make any changes to the way things were done in the surgery was worrying, especially if it was bound up with loyalty to her dead husband. However, what really upset him was the thought of her disappointment at not being allowed to have a child of her own.

It seemed wrong to him that a woman who was as caring and as committed as Helen should be denied the one thing she wanted most of all. It also made him feel incredibly helpless to know there was nothing he could do to help her.

CHAPTER THREE

'THE next case is an interesting one. The patient's name is Ben Harmon. He's a farmer and two months ago he had a serious accident while he was ploughing one of his fields.'

Helen withdrew Ben Harmon's file from her case and handed it to Lewis then started the car. They were onto their fifth call of the day and the anger she'd felt in the surgery still hadn't abated. She could scarcely believe that he'd had the temerity to tell her how she should run the practice after he'd been there for just one week. Why on earth did he think that he knew more about running the place than she did?

'I'm sorry. I shouldn't have said what I did at the surgery. You have every right to be annoyed with me.'

The apology caught her unawares so that the car swerved towards the ditch. Helen's mouth compressed as she quickly righted it. She hated to feel so vulnerable. Lewis was the new partner in the practice—an incomer, as the people of Summerfield would have called him—and he shouldn't have this effect on her. She had to nip these foolish feelings in the bud.

'I'm not annoyed. You're entitled to voice your opinion, just as I am entitled to veto any ideas I feel aren't appropriate.'

'Good.'

'Good?' She shot him a wary glance, taking care to keep her attention on the road this time. Fortunately, there was very little traffic about so there'd been no danger of her causing an accident earlier. However, she liked to be in control of everything she did, whether it was driving a car, diagnosing a patient or choosing a lover.

The last thought made her gasp and she bit her lip, hoping that he hadn't heard the revealing little sound. She had never entertained such a salacious thought in the whole of her life and couldn't understand why it had occurred to her now. It smacked of desperation and…and sexual frustration, and she could feel herself growing hot at the idea it was that which had prompted it.

The strange thing was that sex had never been that important to her. She'd had very little experience when she'd married Ian and their sex life had been rather disappointing at first until she'd realised that the bells and whistles she'd read about in books only happened in fiction, not real life. Once she had adjusted to the realities of married life, she'd grown to appreciate the feeling of closeness that love-making had engendered, and realised it was worth far more than the wild passion that was the staple of all those romance novels. However, that didn't explain why it suddenly felt as though she'd been missing something.

'What do you mean by "good"?' she demanded, furious with him as well as with herself for getting carried away by such a foolish notion.

'I meant it's good that you aren't annoyed and that you welcome input from your staff,' he replied with a calm that merely highlighted her own waspishness.

'I am always open to new ideas,' she told him between gritted teeth. 'However, as I made clear before, I shall decide how the surgery should be run.'

'And whoever works there will just have to fit in.'

His tone was bland so she couldn't blame that for the fact that she felt a bit ridiculous all of a sudden. It was completely contrary to her nature to lay down the law, yet that's what she'd done both now and earlier on in the staffroom. She was sorely tempted to apologise for her behaviour, only she wasn't sure if it would be wise to show any sign of weakness in front of him. It was a relief when he changed the subject by asking her about the patient they were about to visit.

'I think I mentioned that Ben was ploughing when the accident happened,' she explained in a deliberately neutral tone. 'He ploughed up some old oildrums which had been dumped in one of the fields, and when he got off the tractor to see what they contained, he ended up inhaling a massive dose of raw chromium fumes.'

'How on earth did drums of chromium get into his field?'

'Nobody knows.' Helen shrugged. 'The police are still investigating, but they think it might have been waste from the local tannery. It closed down a couple of years ago and the police are trying to trace the owners.'

'I see. So what happened to Mr Harmon as a result of the accident?'

'There was some damage to his nasal passages but the ENT specialist has sorted that out now. The real problem has been the burns on his arms. He's been seeing a plastic surgeon at the local hospital so today I want to check how he's progressing.'

'So this visit isn't because he's actually ill?'

'No. But it's our policy to follow up on a patient, as I explained at your interview,' she said, trying not to bridle at the implied criticism.

'I remember. I also recall telling you that it was a policy I'd adopted myself. However, when I saw patients following their surgery, it was because I was still responsible for their care. If you've passed this patient over to a consultant, I would have thought your part in the proceedings had ended.'

'Follow-up care doesn't come with a cut-off point. I was and still am Ben Harmon's first point of call for any future medical treatment. I like to be fully prepared so I know what I might be dealing with.'

'An admirable sentiment but also a luxury few GPs can afford. Most are happy to hand over a patient to someone else to free up their time.'

'Then that's obviously where I differ from most GPs. I take my responsibilities to my patients very seriously,' she shot back, stung into replying with more vigour than she'd intended.

'Maybe too seriously,' he suggested, his voice grating in a way that made the hairs on the back of her neck spring to attention.

Helen didn't reply, afraid that if she said anything it might be too revealing. Letting him know about the power he had over her would be a mistake and she knew it, too. However, her silence didn't appear to deter him, as she'd hoped it would.

'There's no doubt that you're totally committed to the welfare of your patients, Helen, but is it right that you should put them first all the time and yourself second?'

'I have no idea what—'

'I'm talking about,' he finished for her. 'And that just makes it worse. You obviously can't see that it's wrong to work yourself into the ground the way you're doing, and wrong to devote every waking minute to your job.'

He placed his hand on her arm and she had to make a conscious effort not to react when she felt the warmth of his fingers seeping into her skin. 'When was the last time you took a holiday, for instance?'

'That's none of your business,' she retorted, shrugging off his hand because if she allowed it to remain there she'd want to feel it on other parts of her body as well.

The thought was too much, coming on top of all the others. She drew up at the side of the road and turned to glare at him. 'How dare you pass judgement on how I choose to conduct my life? You've been at the surgery for less than a week yet you seem to think that you know everything about me.'

'It wasn't difficult to formulate a fairly clear picture of your life.'

He didn't back down, certainly didn't apologise, and her heart spasmed in fear because she wasn't sure if she was up to winning this argument. Reaching for the handbrake, she went to set off again but this time his hand closed over hers, hard and firm as he stopped her.

'Your life can be summed up in one word, Helen: work. While it might be admirable to show a certain degree of dedication, you are taking it to extremes, and that isn't good for you or the rest of the staff. A good manager leads by example.'

'Thank you for that advice, Dr Cole. However, this isn't London and while your theories might work there they don't apply here. I don't have the luxury of a team of staff at my beck and call. If I didn't put one hundred per cent effort into my job, we wouldn't be able to keep the practice running.'

'Which is why it's so important to cut down on any unnecessary work. The whole appointment system needs to be streamlined and made more selective. That way everyone will benefit. Patients who need extra care will get it and the staff won't be run ragged, trying to do everything.'

'Nobody else has complained. Maybe they are more used to hard work than you are.'

'And maybe they don't want to make your life any more difficult. Everyone can see that you're doing too much, Helen. You need to ease off and find some outside interests. Working the number of hours that you do isn't good for anyone.'

'I'm not listening to any more,' she murmured, but he ignored her and carried on stripping away her defences as though they were tissue thin.

'You're the first to arrive each morning and the last to leave each night. Even on Sunday, when I drove past the surgery to show Kristy where I would be working, your car was parked outside. Despite what you might think, I worked damned hard in my last post, but I knew when I needed to take time off and I took it. It makes me very sad to think that you haven't anything better to do with your life apart from work.'

He let go of her hand and she shrank back in her seat when he touched her lightly on the cheek because the feel of his fingers on her skin was every bit as potent as she'd imagined it would be.

'You deserve more than a life that's comprised solely of work, Helen.'

* * *

'So how do you feel today, Mr Harmon?'

'A lot better than I did.' The young farmer smiled wryly. 'I really thought my number was up when I breathed in those fumes. If it hadn't been for Polly, it might have been, too.'

'Polly?' Lewis made a conscious effort to appear interested. Maybe it wouldn't make up for what he'd done by telling Helen that her life was a mess, but it might make him feel a bit better.

'The dog.' Ben Harmon put his hand on the German shepherd's head. The animal responded immediately, looking up at him with adoring eyes, and Lewis felt even worse.

Helen most certainly wouldn't look at him like that in the foreseeable future! In fact, he wouldn't be surprised if she told him that he no longer had a job when they left the farm. The thought of the disruption it would cause to Kristy's life if they had to move again was more than he could face and he silently cursed himself.

'It was Polly's barking that alerted everyone, you see.'

'Really?' He forced himself to concentrate on what the farmer was saying. 'It's a good job she was with you.'

'You can say that again. I'd have had it if Dad hadn't heard the commotion Polly was making and come to see what was going on. I'd passed out by then, overcome by the fumes from those containers. Dad managed to drag me out of the way and phoned the surgery.'

Ben glanced at Helen and chuckled. 'Dr Daniels soon got me sorted out. She drove me to hospital and rushed me straight through to the emergency unit. It's all a bit hazy but I remember the fuss she made when some young doctor foolishly tried to stop her. Folk round here know better than to get in her way when she's on a mission!'

Lewis joined in when Ben laughed but his spirits had sunk to an all-time low. Obviously, Helen was highly regarded in the town because of her dedication, yet he'd had the nerve to criticise her. Taking a pair of gloves out of his case, he mentally rehearsed what he would say to her later if she gave him the chance to apologise. Even though he stood by what he'd said about the way she ran the practice, maybe it hadn't been his place to point it out.

'I'd like to take a look at your arms,' he explained. 'I see from your notes that the district nurse has been to visit you but I'd like to check how they're healing.'

'It's taken a bit of time to get this far,' Ben admitted as Lewis gently peeled away the dressings. 'The doctor I saw at the hospital wasn't sure if there'd been some other chemicals mixed in with the chromium, possibly some kind of acid.'

'They look very much like acid burns to me.' He glanced at Helen, doing his best to slip back into his old persona. The cool, efficient surgeon was a role he'd played for many years and he sensed that she would respond better if he adopted it again. It was when she thought he was getting too close that the problems began.

The thought stunned him. It had never occurred to him before that Helen's prickliness might stem from her feelings towards him. He had to make a conscious effort to continue. 'What do you think, Helen? Do they look like acid burns to you?'

'Very much so. There was a similar incident a couple of years ago when another drum of chemicals was found in a ditch. One of the boys who found it was badly burnt when the acid leaked onto his feet.'

Her tone was professional to a fault and he breathed a sigh of relief. Of course she would feel duty bound to respond in front of a patient but at least she was speaking to him, and that was something.

'Did the consultant at the hospital suggest plastic surgery?' he asked, turning to the farmer again.

'He did, although I'm not sure if I fancy the idea.' Ben grimaced. 'He said something about taking skin from my thighs to cover the burns, but that would mean I'd have two lots of scars instead of just one.'

'The plastic surgeons are very good so any scarring on your legs would be hardly noticeable. But it's your decision so don't let yourself be talked into it if it isn't what you want. The flesh is healing so I'd guess the consultant suggested it for cosmetic reasons.'

'It would be all right if I refused, then?' Ben looked a bit sheepish. 'I'm hopeless when it comes to anyone in authority. I never stand up for myself and say what I want. I just go along with whatever they suggest.'

'Of course you can refuse!' Lewis patted him on the shoulder. 'Every patient has the right to refuse treatment so don't let yourself be railroaded into doing something you aren't happy about.'

'Well, if you think it would be all right, I'll tell the doctor that I'd rather not bother.' Ben sounded relieved. 'I don't want to be laid up any longer than necessary when it means my dad has to do all the work. You get a lot of knocks when you're farming so a few extra scars aren't going to make much difference to me!'

'That's one way to look at it.' Lewis laughed. 'Right, I think that's it... Unless there's anything you want to check, Helen,' he added politely.

'No. Everything seems to be progressing very nicely from what I've seen today.' She smiled at the young farmer. 'Don't forget that you can ring me any time, Ben. You have my home phone number so you don't need to go through the on-call service if it's after surgery hours.'

'Thanks, Dr Daniels. I really appreciate that.'

Ben saw them out, putting a restraining hand on the dog's head when it tried to follow them to the car. Lewis fastened his seat belt, taking care not to look at Helen as she got in beside him. He couldn't believe what he'd heard. Helen handed out her private phone number and told patients to call her at home rather than use the on-call service?

He sat in silence as they drove back to town. The situation was far worse than he'd imagined it to be, yet what could he do about it? By the time they arrived back at the surgery, he was seething with frustration. Stalking into his room, he tossed his case onto the desk with a thud that reverberated around the room. Amy happened to be passing and she stopped.

'Everything OK, Lewis?'

'Fine,' he snapped, then sighed when he saw her start of surprise. 'Sorry. I didn't mean to snap at you. I'm just so bloody furious with Helen. She must be mad!'

'Not a word I'd normally use to describe her,' Amy said wryly, coming into the room. 'Come on, tell me what's happened now.'

'I just found out that Helen has been telling patients to phone her at home if they have a problem outside surgery hours.'

'Really?' Amy whistled. 'She's kept that very quiet because I had no idea. Oh, I know she wasn't keen on hiring an on-call service. It took us months to convince her that she couldn't keep going out to visit patients every night and still do her job during the day. But I honestly thought she'd accepted the idea by now.'

'It didn't sound like it from what I heard.' He thrust an impatient hand through his hair, wondering why he was getting so steamed up. It was up to Helen what she did, yet he couldn't accept that it was none of his business when she was in serious danger of running herself into the ground. 'How long have you been using an on-call service?'

'About a year. Ian refused to use one when he was alive and I think that was why we had such difficulty persuading Helen to sign up.' Amy shrugged. 'It's the old story, I'm afraid—what Ian decided is still law around here.'

'But can't she see that it's time she moved on?' he exploded. He swung round and walked to the window so that Amy couldn't see how frustrated he felt. He didn't want her to start wondering why he was so concerned about Helen's working habits when he couldn't explain it himself. He just knew it was wrong for her to be living this way.

'I know it must have been awful for her to be widowed so

young,' he said over his shoulder. 'But it's time she got over it. And clinging to her dead husband's beliefs isn't the way to do it.'

'Lewis,' Amy said anxiously, but he ignored her, needing to vent the frustration that had been building up inside him all day.

'She seems to be stuck in some sort of a time warp. That's why we're using such an outdated appointment system. It's as though the world stopped when her husband died, but she needs to understand that it's time she moved on!'

He glanced round, wondering if he'd said too much, and felt a jolt of alarm hit him when he saw how embarrassed Amy looked. Maybe his remarks had been a little too revealing?

A movement by the door attracted his attention and he turned. Helen was standing outside the room and he knew immediately that she'd heard every word. Her eyes met his for a second and his heart sank when he saw the pain they held. However, before he could attempt to make amends, she hurried away.

'Oh, dear!'

Amy looked really upset as she quickly left the room. Lewis sympathised with her. He felt dreadful, too. He had just taken everything that Helen held dear and rubbished it. He didn't think he would ever get over the way she'd looked at him just now—so wounded and betrayed.

He sat down at his desk and put his head in his hands. What had he done?

Helen went straight to her room. There was a buzzing in her head and her legs were trembling. Walking over to the handbasin, she sluiced her face with cold water but the feelings didn't subside.

She sat down at her desk, wondering what she was going to do. She had to do something, of course. She couldn't let Lewis get away with what he'd said. She had to make him understand that he was wrong about her...

Only he wasn't.

She had been stuck in a time warp since Ian had died. She'd been clinging to the past because the future terrified her. What did she have to look forward to? She was a widow of thirty-eight with two grown-up stepchildren and a demanding job.

That was it. There was nothing more, nothing for herself, the woman she was inside, a woman who once had dreamed of having a child of her own and someone to love her for all eternity. Lewis was right—she *did* devote every waking minute to her job. But what else did she have?

'I'm sorry you overheard that. I had no right to say what I did and I certainly had no right to involve Amy. Those were my views and they had nothing whatsoever to do with her.'

Helen's head shot up when she recognised Lewis's voice. All the fear and frustration she was feeling suddenly seemed to combine into one potent force and she rounded on him.

'It's customary to knock before you enter a room. Or don't you believe the rules which most civilised people live by apply to you, Dr Cole?'

'I did knock. Obviously, you didn't hear me.'

He came over to her desk and there was something in his eyes that made her anger suddenly pale in the face of all the other emotions she was experiencing. She didn't want him looking at her as though he cared. She couldn't afford to let herself believe that he was interested in her. The only thing he was interested in was getting his own way!

She shot to her feet. 'No, I didn't hear you. I was too busy working out what I was going to say to you.'

'And have you decided?' he asked, his voice grating so that her hands clenched when she felt another rush of awareness hit her.

'Yes.'

There was no way that she was prepared to give in to these feelings and let him gain the upper hand. She was in charge of this practice and she wouldn't allow anyone to overrule her. Her job was all she had and the thought made her feel more mixed up than ever, only she couldn't afford to let him know how painful the idea was. She looked him squarely in the eye because the best way she knew to resolve this problem was by meeting it head on.

'You had no right to discuss me with anyone. I will not permit you to make personal remarks about the way I choose to live my life. If you cannot accept that then I'm afraid I shall have no choice other than to demand your resignation.'

CHAPTER FOUR

KRISTY was very quiet on the way home from the after-school club that night but Lewis didn't try to draw her out as he usually did. He was too busy thinking about what Helen had said to him.

He didn't want to have to tender his resignation so from now on he would be far more careful about what he said. He also didn't want to upset her again and it was worrying to know that he was so concerned about her feelings when she'd made it clear that she didn't care about his. He tried not to dwell on the thought as he drew up in front of the house. He spent far too little time with Kristy as it was and it wasn't fair to spend it worrying about his problems.

'Would you like to watch a video after we've had our tea, sweetheart?' he asked, smiling at the little girl.

'All right,' she mumbled, avoiding his eyes as she scrambled out of the car.

Lewis sighed as he followed her to the house. She was always so distant with him and he only wished that he could find a way to break down the barriers she'd erected around herself. He knew he must be patient if he hoped to gain her trust, but he would have loved to receive the occasional positive response from her.

'Can I go and see the horse?' she asked as soon as they were inside.

'Yes, but put your schoolbag away first.'

He went into the kitchen and opened the refrigerator as she

ran off down the hall. He'd not had time to go shopping since they'd arrived so there wasn't much choice. They'd fallen into the habit of buying a take-away supper every Friday in London and he suddenly decided that they would continue the practice. Kristy might appreciate the familiar routine and he would definitely appreciate a night free from cooking!

He went to the back door and told Kristy they were going out to buy their supper. She was reluctant to leave the horse, although she didn't object, and once again he found himself wishing that she would show a little more spirit. Maybe some parents would be delighted by such unquestioning obedience but it troubled him. She should be making her opinions known instead of passively agreeing to everything he suggested.

It made him see how much work he still had to do to forge a bond between them, and how silly it would be to involve himself any more in Helen's affairs. He needed to concentrate on his daughter and forget everything else.

'Just leave everything in the tray, Janet, and get off home. It's far too late to do the filing now.'

Helen sighed as the receptionist thanked her and hurriedly left. It was almost a quarter to seven—way past the time they were supposed to finish. Everyone else had left some time ago but she'd slotted a couple of extra patients into her list when they'd turned up without appointments. She could have refused to see them, but Ian had drummed it into her that the patients came first and that their own needs came a very poor second.

She frowned as she switched off the waiting-room lights. She'd never given any thought to that theory before, yet all of a sudden she found herself wondering if it was the right approach. Obviously, the patients deserved the highest level of care but was it really necessary to sacrifice their private lives to achieve that? Surely there should be a better balance between the needs of the patients and the needs of the staff—as Lewis had pointed out.

Her mouth compressed as she made her way to her room.

Maybe she did need to make some changes to the way the surgery was run, but she didn't need Lewis to advise her. He could keep his opinions to himself from now on. And if he couldn't do so then he would soon discover that she hadn't been making an idle threat when she'd promised to fire him!

She felt a little better after reconfirming her decision to put a stop to his meddling. Sitting down at her desk, she set to work on the following year's budget. The primary health care trust was demanding more cuts and it wasn't easy to find an area where she could make any reductions to their spending. When the phone rang, she automatically picked up the receiver before the answering-machine could cut in.

'Helen Daniels. Can I help you?'

'It's Lucy, Dr Daniels…Lucy Maguire,' a worried voice announced.

Helen frowned as she put down her pen. Lucy was a frequent visitor to the surgery. A single mother with two boisterous children to care for, she was always calling in with one child or the other. Helen was well acquainted with her circumstances and knew that Lucy had been finding it difficult to cope since she'd moved back to Summerfield after her partner had left her.

'Hello, Lucy. What's happened now?'

'It's Josh. He tripped over and banged his head on the hearth. He's not moving and I don't know what to do!'

'Just try to stay calm,' Helen told her firmly when she heard the panic in the young mother's voice. 'Have you phoned for an ambulance?'

'No. I didn't know if I should…'

'That's OK. I'll do it for you. Now, can you check if Josh is breathing? Put your ear against his chest and see if you can hear the air going in and out of his lungs.'

'I'll try.' Lucy dropped the receiver, and came back a minute later. 'Yes, I can hear him breathing.'

'That's excellent. What I want you to do next, Lucy, is to roll him over and lay him on his side. That way he won't choke if he's sick. Use some cushions or a couple of pillows to prop him up if he's a bit floppy. '

'I'll do it now, Dr Daniels.'

Helen waited while Lucy followed her instructions. She carried on as soon as Lucy came back on the line. 'I want you to stay with Josh until I get there. If he wakes up, just keep him calm. He mustn't start running around.'

'I'll try,' Lucy said anxiously. 'But Josh can be very difficult at times.'

'Just do your best and I'll be there very shortly.'

Helen hung up. There was no point wasting time by explaining that a three-year-old child shouldn't be dictating what he would and wouldn't do. Lucy had a hard enough time as it was, without *her* preaching.

She phoned for an ambulance then locked up, hesitating before she set the alarm. She was too tired to concentrate on the budget again that night so she wouldn't come back after she'd seen Lucy. It meant she would have to finish the paperwork over the weekend—not that she had anything better planned.

She'd started to dread the weekends since the twins had left for Australia. The time seemed to drag now that she was on her own so for the past few weekends she'd come into work. There was always something that needed doing, although she wouldn't want Lewis to know she was planning another stint that weekend. He'd made it perfectly clear what he thought of her working habits!

Lewis was on his way home with fish and chips for their supper when he spotted Helen coming out of a house in the centre of the town. There was an ambulance parked outside and he could see one of the paramedics opening the back doors. Although he was wary about interfering after what had gone on earlier in the day, he couldn't just drive past. Anyway, Helen might be less prickly away from the surgery when she wouldn't feel as though her authority was being threatened.

He drew up and turned to Kristy. 'I just need to see what's happened, sweetheart, so you stay here for a moment. I won't be long.'

'OK.'

He sighed when he heard the lack of interest in her voice. He really needed to find a way to rouse her from her inertia, he thought as he got out of the car. Helen was ushering the paramedics inside but she stopped when she saw him crossing the pavement.

'What are you doing here?'

'I spotted the ambulance as I was passing. Do you need a hand?'

'No, thank you very much. I can manage—'

She broke off when a scream suddenly erupted from inside the house. Lewis didn't wait for permission as he hurriedly followed her indoors and took in the scene that greeted him. There was a small boy lying on the floor, being violently sick. Another child was staring at him, wide-eyed with terror, while the mother was screaming hysterically.

'Can you deal with Mum while I deal with the child?' he instructed, hurrying over to the boy. He didn't pause to wonder if Helen would be annoyed about him taking charge and, surprisingly, she didn't object.

'His name's Josh and he's three. Apparently, he fell over and hit his head on the hearth. He lost consciousness for a short time, although he was conscious when I got here.' She passed him her case. 'You'll need this. I haven't had time to examine him properly yet.'

'Thanks.' Lewis knelt down as she hurried over to the mother. The paramedics were mopping the little boy up and he waited until they'd finished before he attempted to examine him. 'There's no need to be scared, son. I'm a doctor and I just want to make you feel better.'

'I want my mummy,' the little boy whimpered.

'Mummy's right there with Dr Daniels. She's a bit upset so why don't I check that you're all right before we call her over?'

The child thought about it for a moment then solemnly nodded. Lewis smiled at him. 'That's a really brave boy. Now, first of all, can you tell me your name?'

'Joshua Peter Maguire,' the child replied importantly.

'That's very good. And do you know how old you are, Joshua?'

'Three!'

'Three?' Lewis whistled. 'I thought you were a lot older than that.'

He opened the case, took out a small torch and showed it to the child. Now that he'd established that Josh could remember his name and his age, it was time to check for any other signs of a head injury. He switched on the torch and shone it on the back of the little boy's hand.

'I'm going to shine this little light into your eyes to check that they're working properly. There's nothing to be scared about—OK?'

Josh sat perfectly still while Lewis checked his pupils. Lewis ruffled his hair as he turned off the torch. 'I wish all my patients were as good as you are, Josh.'

He turned to the paramedics. 'Both pupils are dilating evenly so I think we can rule out a serious head injury. However, in view of the fact that he lost consciousness and has vomited, I think it would be safer if he was admitted to hospital for observation.'

He left the paramedics to deal with the transfer and went over to where Helen was sitting beside the boy's mother. The woman had her arm round the other child and he could see that she was trembling violently when he crouched down in front of her.

'Josh seems to be fine but I think it would be best if he's admitted to hospital overnight.'

'Hospital!' the woman exclaimed in dismay.

'It's for his own good, Lucy,' Helen put in, quickly backing him up. 'Josh lost consciousness and he's been sick so he might have a mild concussion. It would be much safer if he was in hospital so they can monitor him.'

'Well, if you think it's really necessary,' Lucy agreed hesitantly.

'We do.' Lewis smiled at her, hoping that Helen wouldn't mind him speaking for her as well. 'There's no point taking any chances, is there?'

'No, of course not.' Lucy took a steadying breath then stood up. 'I'd better pack a few bits and pieces that he'll need.'

It took just a few minutes for the paramedics to load the child into the ambulance. Lewis knew that he didn't need to wait but he was loath to leave before he'd had a word with Helen. Maybe this wasn't the ideal time to try and make his peace with her but he couldn't think of a better one.

'Thanks for everything, Dr Daniels. I'm really sorry to have called you out. I should have phoned for an ambulance instead of ringing the surgery, but I get so scared when anything happens to one of the boys.'

Lewis didn't hear what Helen said—he was too busy thinking about what he'd heard. He hadn't given any thought to how Helen had come to be at the house, but now it struck him that she must have responded to the call instead of allowing their on-call service to take it. And once again he found his frustration spilling over.

'How come you took the call?' he demanded as she came over to him. 'The on-call service should have deal with it.'

'I happened to be in the surgery when Lucy phoned.' A wash of guilty colour ran up her cheeks but she stood her ground. 'Not that it's any of your business. We already agreed that it isn't your place to comment on what I do, Dr Cole.'

'I didn't agree to anything. You told me to mind my own business and threatened me with the sack if I didn't do so.'

'Then obviously you must care very little about your position at The Beeches,' she snapped back, unlocking her car and tossing her case into the back.

'Oh, I care all right.' He stepped forward and blocked her way when she went to open the driver's door. 'I don't want to lose this job for several reasons—first of all because it would disrupt Kristy's life if we had to move again and secondly because I enjoy working here. However, I can't just stand by and watch you working yourself into an early grave.'

'Why not?' She laughed scornfully. 'What possible difference does it make to you what I do?'

Lewis winced. Helen obviously thought he was meddling for some unknown reasons of his own but that couldn't be further from the truth. He wanted her to understand the mistake she was making for her own good, although it didn't seem a good idea to tell her that.

'Because you're setting a dangerous precedent, Helen. If you keep responding to calls after hours, the patients will expect everyone to do the same. It isn't fair to expect us all to give up our free time.'

'I see. Then I must apologise for putting you in such a difficult position. I shall make it clear that I am the only person who should be contacted in an emergency.'

'And you really think that's the answer?' It was hard to hide his dismay so he didn't try. 'Come on, Helen, that's just plain stupid. You pay for an on-call service so use it! You deserve more out of life than always being at the beck and call of your patients.'

'I am perfectly happy with my life the way it is,' she told him, coldly enunciating every word.

Lewis knew that if he hadn't been watching her so closely, he might have believed that claim. However, he saw the pain that flickered in her eyes and knew it was a lie. His voice softened because he didn't want to scare her when it appeared he might be making a breakthrough at last.

'Then you're very lucky. There aren't many people who are completely satisfied with their lot. Most folk would like to make a few changes to their lives. I know I would.'

'Then my advice is to concentrate on your own problems and leave me alone.'

She wrenched open the car door, forcing him to step back as she slid into the driver's seat. Lewis knew that she was going to drive away and knew, too, that he would lose the small advantage he'd gained if he let her. He'd made a little headway and he needed to capitalise on it while he could.

'Look, Helen, I'm sorry. Again!'

His tone was wry, the shrug he gave when she glanced at him filled with contrition. Maybe the apology wasn't one hundred per cent genuine but he would square that with his conscience later. Right now it was more important that he didn't let her solder up that chink that had appeared in her armour.

He crouched down so that their faces were level, feeling his heart squeeze in an extra beat when he inhaled the fragrance of her skin. It wasn't perfume he could smell but her own natural scent, and it was doing all sorts of crazy things to his libido. However, that wasn't the issue at the moment, he reminded himself sternly. He wasn't trying to seduce her. He was trying to make her see sense so any feelings of a less than altruistic nature had to be put on hold.

'I know I've apologised more times than you can count today but I'm truly sorry for upsetting you.' Deliberately, he tried to inject a touch of concern into his voice and was surprised when he discovered how easy it was to strike the right note. 'Will you forgive me?'

'Well…'

She wavered and he hurried on because it was essential that she didn't go storming off. If she had a whole weekend to think about what he'd said, she would find a reason not to believe him. And he simply wasn't prepared to let that happen.

'Please?'

'Oh, I suppose so.'

She gave him a grudging smile and his spirits soared for a moment before the complexities of the situation hit him. He'd done what he'd set out to do and had stopped her driving off, but what should he do now? He still hadn't cleared the air properly and he really needed to do that, only this wasn't the best time when Kristy was waiting in the car for him.

He came to a swift decision, prompted by necessity rather

than choice. If the circumstances had been different, he would have suggested that they find some place quiet where they could talk. However, being a father meant he had responsibilities and it wasn't possible to do that.

'I've just been to the fish-and-chip shop for our supper. I always buy far too much so why don't you come back home with us?' He grinned at her, wanting to reassure her in case she still had doubts about his motives. 'Apart from the fact it will prove that you've forgiven me for poking my nose into your affairs, Kristy will get the chance to meet you. She's waiting in the car for me right now, as it happens.'

'I don't know if I should...' Helen glanced across the road and he could sense her indecision when she saw the little girl. 'We've said everything that needs to be said.'

'I know. But I just want to make sure that everything is sorted out.' He treated her to his most engaging smile. 'We can eat our supper while I apologise again, and if that isn't a big enough inducement, I'll see if I can rustle up a slice of humble pie for afters!'

She laughed at that, a lilting sound that did horrendous things to his composure. Images suddenly began to flicker behind his eyes, pictures of him and Helen sitting close together on his sofa—laughing, kissing...

No!

He dragged his mind back from such a tempting path and piled on the pressure. They desperately needed to resolve their differences if they were to work together. 'Kristy will be really upset if you refuse. She's been longing to meet you ever since we got here.'

Helen sighed. 'You can be very persuasive when you want to be, Lewis. If I don't agree, I'll feel guilty about refusing to meet her.'

'So is that a yes?'

'Yes, all right.' She slid the key into the ignition then looked up at him. 'I'll follow you back, shall I?'

'Yes. Fine. Great.'

He stood up abruptly and went back to his car. It was just a five-minute drive to Mill Cottage and it wasn't nearly long enough to calm himself down. As he drew up in front of the house, he could feel his heart pounding inside his chest—bang, bang, bang. Like a steamhammer working overtime. He knew he was right to try to resolve this issue between him and Helen, but he hadn't considered the repercussions it could have. When she'd looked at him just now he'd seen such yearning in her eyes that it had woken an answering need inside him.

He knew how easy it would be to give in to these feelings but it would be the wrong thing to do. He could never give Helen what she really needed. He couldn't offer her a future because he'd promised that to Kristy and he would never let his daughter down.

CHAPTER FIVE

'CAN I do anything to help?'

Helen looked around the kitchen, wondering if she'd been mad to accept Lewis's invitation. He'd already apologised for his interference so why had she let him persuade her to come back to his home? Was it really so important that she got to know his daughter?

Her gaze moved to the little girl and she felt her heart ache in a way it hadn't done for ages. She'd thought she'd reconciled herself to never having a child of her own yet she couldn't help feeling wistful as she watched Kristy arrange the cutlery on the table. There'd been a huge gap in her life since the twins had left home, but she mustn't make the mistake of seeing Kristy as a substitute for them.

The thought startled her. Lewis had never even hinted that he would welcome her help in caring for his daughter so she had no idea where it had sprung from. It was hard to hide her dismay when he glanced round.

'Could you fetch the glasses?' He pointed to the huge old Welsh dresser at the far end of the room. 'We use the ones on the top shelf and Kristy can't reach them, can you, poppet?'

'No.'

The little girl didn't look up when he spoke to her. Helen frowned as she went to the dresser and took three brightly patterned glass tumblers off the shelf. It wasn't unusual for a child that age to be shy around strangers, but Kristy's response to her father had been strangely subdued since they'd got back to the house. Helen couldn't fault the way Lewis had spoken to her— every word had been laced with affection. Yet not once had he received any kind of positive reaction and it bothered Helen in a way she couldn't explain.

'We're just about ready… Oops! I forgot the ketchup. Silly me.' Lewis grinned at his daughter as he set the plates on the table. 'We can't have fish and chips without tomato ketchup, can we, sweetie?'

'No.'

Once again his question was met with a single-word answer, and Helen's unease deepened. As she sat down at the table, she couldn't help wondering if Lewis realised how odd it was for a child to act this way. He'd admitted during his interview that it had been a shock to discover that he was a father so maybe he thought it was normal behaviour.

'Salt, vinegar, ketchup… I think that's it now so tuck in.' He took his seat, smiling at her across the table. 'Friday night is take-away night so that's my excuse for a calorie-laden meal. The rest of the week we try to be good, don't we, Kristy?'

'Uh-huh.'

The little girl kept her eyes on her plate and Helen frowned. There was definitely something odd going on, although she wasn't sure what exactly it was.

'This is a real treat for me,' she said, addressing the little girl to see if she could get a reaction from her. 'Normally, I'm very strict with myself and stick to all the healthy things you're supposed to eat. Lots of fruit and vegetables—things like that.'

'That's what my mommy eats,' Kristy said, glancing shyly at her. 'She said that if she'd gotten fat then Joe wouldn't love her any more.'

Helen wasn't sure what to say in reply and glanced at Lewis for guidance. Her heart sank when she saw the pain on his face.

It was obvious the comment had upset him, although she had no idea why. Unless he was jealous at the thought of Kristy's mother wanting to look nice for another man?

It was difficult to hide how dismayed she felt by that idea but she knew it would be wrong to let him know the effect it had had on her. She didn't look in his direction as she smiled at Kristy again. 'Most women like to look nice. I know I do so that's one of the reasons why I don't eat fish and chips very often. But they are delicious as a treat, aren't they?'

'I like pizza best.' Kristy gave her the ghost of a smile. 'With pepperoni sausage on it.'

'Oh, yum! So do I. And lots of cheese.' Helen patted her tummy. 'Scrummy!'

Kristy burst out laughing. 'That's a funny word.'

'What? Scrummy?' Helen dunked a chip into the puddle of ketchup on the side of her plate. 'It means all lovely and delicious, doesn't it, Lewis?'

She deliberately included him in the conversation because it would appear more normal if she did so. Her heart jolted once again when she saw the pain that lingered in his eyes before he made an obvious effort to collect himself.

'That's right. It's a great word, too. Did you have a word like it to describe the things you liked when you were living in Miami, darling?'

'Can't remember.'

Kristy's face closed up as she bent over her plate again. Helen looked at Lewis in surprise but he just shrugged. They finished their supper but even though he kept up a lively conversation about the highs and lows of moving from the city, she could hear the strain in his voice. It bothered her so much that as soon as Kristy had been despatched to the sitting-room to watch a cartoon, she asked him what was going on.

'Where do I begin?' he said ruefully, gathering together their dirty plates to take them to the sink.

'The beginning is usually the best place,' she replied lightly, picking up the glasses. Turning on the tap, she filled the wash-ing-up bowl with hot water.

'You don't have to do the dishes. You're supposed to be our guest.'

'Washing a few dishes isn't going to kill me.' She added a squirt of detergent to the water then plunged the glasses into the suds. 'So what's wrong with Kristy?'

'I wish I knew. I've tried everything I can think of to get her to open up but she just clams up.' He picked up a teatowel and started to dry the dishes. 'Tonight was the first time I've heard her mention her mother and it was you she spoke to about Tessa, not me.'

'Sorry.' Helen sighed. 'I didn't mean to step on your toes.'

'You didn't—just the opposite, in fact.' He tossed the teatowel onto the counter in a fit of impatience. 'Kristy needs to talk about what happened in Miami. I know that and I've also been told it by the experts I've consulted.'

'Experts?' she repeated in surprise.

'Yes. I was worried about how I would fare when I brought Kristy back to England so I had a word with one of the child psy-chologists at St Leona's. I'd never had much to do with kids be-fore Kristy came into my life and I wanted to know how best to deal with any problems she might have, settling down in a new country.' He grimaced. 'Rather naïve of me to think it was that simple, wasn't it? The psychologist explained there are no hard-and-fast rules in a situation like this. He advised me to talk to her about her past experiences, but she clams up whenever I men-tion Tessa.'

'Have you thought of taking her to see someone…another child psychologist, I mean?'

'Yes, I've thought about it. She did receive counselling while she was in care but I was told it didn't achieve very much. She wouldn't talk about what had happened to her, and refused to speak about her mother.' He sighed. 'I know that we need to deal with the problem but I'm not sure if sending her for counselling again is the right thing to do at the moment. She's painfully shy with strangers and it would mean putting her through another ordeal. Basically, I'm just feeling my way and taking each day as it comes.'

'It can't be easy for you, though,' she said softly, and he sighed.

'I think frustrated sums up how I feel most of the time. I just can't seem to get through to her. It's as though she's put up this wall and I'm on one side and she's on the other. As I said, tonight was the first time she's mentioned Tessa. And to hear her speak about Tessa in the same breath as that man…!'

He broke off, obviously not wanting to vent his anger in front of her. Helen's heart sank because it seemed she'd been right in her assessment. Lewis was jealous at the thought of Tessa and the other man, and for some reason it was upsetting to see the proof of it now.

Picking up the teatowel, she briskly dried her hands, refusing to dwell on the idea. Lewis's problems weren't her concern any more than her problems were his. 'Thank you for supper. It was very kind of you to invite me,' she began, only he didn't allow her to finish.

'You're not leaving already? You've not had a cup of coffee yet.'

He picked up the kettle, edging her aside so he could fill it from the tap. Helen felt a ripple of heat run up her arm when his shoulder brushed against hers and bit her lip. The last thing she needed was this kind of complication. Apart from the fact that they were colleagues, Lewis had his daughter to worry about and she had…what?

Her mind raced as she tried to come up with a reason why she shouldn't get to know him better but she couldn't think of anything. She was over the age of consent and single so nobody would think it was wrong if she started dating again. It had been two years since Ian had died so it wasn't as though she could be accused of rushing into anything. Even the twins had hinted that it was time she got on with her life so what was stopping her?

She took a deep breath because it was a lot to contend with. The fact that she'd even considered going out with another man had been a huge step. However, the most shocking thing of all was realising that it was Lewis she wanted to go out with. Was she completely crazy? Or just very, very lonely?

'Help yourself to some more coffee. I won't be long—ten minutes max. This little lady is almost asleep on her feet!'

Lewis cringed when he heard the falsely jovial note in his voice but it was better than letting Helen know how he was really feeling. He ushered Kristy to the door, pausing when Helen said softly behind him, 'I really should go. You must have loads of things to do....'

'I haven't,' he replied brusquely, cursing himself when he saw her start of surprise. He summoned a smile, hoping it would disguise his urgency to keep her there. Maybe it was silly but he didn't want to sit here on his own, thinking about all the mistakes he'd made. He knew it wasn't his fault that Kristy had grown up without him, but he would never forgive himself for what she'd suffered after Tessa had died. Just thinking about the way that guy...Joe...had abandoned her made him want to do something desperate, only it wouldn't help if he lost his sense of proportion. Hopefully, Helen could help him restore it.

It was alarming to realise that he was depending on her to see him through this difficult time and he hurried on. 'The only things I have to do are all the boring jobs, like putting another load of washing into the machine. I'm certainly not in a rush to get them done!'

'In that case, I'll stay a bit longer.' She smiled at him. 'I'll feel guilty if I abandon you to such a dire fate.'

'A true friend,' he replied lightly.

He closed the sitting-room door and followed Kristy up the stairs. He'd let her choose which bedroom she'd wanted when they'd moved in and, unsurprisingly, she'd chosen one at the back. She had a perfect view of the paddock from her window and he smiled when she immediately ran over to it.

'Is the horse still there?' he asked, turning back the quilt.

'Yes.'

She shot a last wistful glance at the object of her affections then obediently came back and climbed into bed. Lewis sighed as she lay down without a murmur. He couldn't help wishing that he'd had to nag or cajole her. All of a sudden he remembered what he and Helen had discussed that morning about Kristy having riding lessons. Maybe that would help to draw her out of her shell?

'You really love that horse, don't you, sweetheart, so how would you like to learn to ride?'

'Ride?' she repeated, staring up at him with huge brown eyes that were the image of her mother's.

Lewis knew that the memory of Tessa had dimmed with time, and it made him feel guilty whenever he was reminded of her. In a way, he wished he could feel more—actually grieve for her—because it might have helped him understand how Kristy was feeling. However, time had taken away any feelings he'd had for her so that all he felt now was sorrow at the waste of her life.

'Daddy?'

He quickly returned his attention to his daughter when he heard the excitement in her voice. It was such a shock to hear her sounding so animated that it was hard not to show how thrilled he felt. 'Yes, sweetie?'

'Did you really mean it about me learning to ride?'

'Of course I did. You like the idea, do you?'

'Oh, yes!'

His heart swelled when he saw the happiness on her face. She looked like a completely different child and he had to stop himself leaping up and shouting for joy. 'Then I'll see if I can book some lessons for you,' he said sedately.

He kissed her on the cheek, not wanting to spoil things by hugging her, as he longed to do, and it was another wonderful surprise when he felt her small arms suddenly wind around his neck. Lewis felt his throat close up with emotion as he gave her a gentle hug then stood up before he committed the sin of clinging to her.

'Night-night. Sleep tight…'

'Mind the bugs don't bite,' she finished for him, and the tears really did flow then because it was another first.

He closed the bedroom door then stood on the landing while he tried to compose himself. Helen was downstairs and he didn't want her to see how moved he was by what had happened. However, when he went back to the sitting-room, it was immediately apparent that she'd noticed something had changed. He sank down onto a chair and let his head fall back against the cushions, knowing it was pointless pretending.

'Kristy just hugged me.'

'And it was the first time it had happened?' she said astutely.

'How did you guess?' His tone was wry and she laughed softly.

'Because I'm too nosy for my own good, I expect.'

'Nosy?' He sat up and stared at her in surprise.

'Mmm.' She gave a little shrug as she reached for her coffee-cup but he could tell that she was embarrassed. 'I was watching you and Kristy tonight and I couldn't help noticing that she avoided making eye contact with you. Sorry. I probably shouldn't have said anything.'

'Why not when it's true?' He sank back against the cushions again, feeling a rush of heat flow through him at the thought of her watching him. It was an effort to keep his thoughts centred but this was more important than anything else. 'As I explained before, Kristy has been very distant towards me since I brought her back from Miami. It's not surprising when she had no real idea who I was, but I can't deny that it's been worrying me.'

'Which is why tonight has been such a boost. What happened to make her respond to you now?'

'I asked her if she'd like to have riding lessons.' His throat closed up again at the memory of his daughter's excitement. It truly had been a red-letter occasion, one that he would remember for the rest of his life.

'I'm really pleased for you.' Helen smiled as she put her cup on the table. 'I know how hard it must have been for you. I went through a similar experience with the twins. They were younger than Kristy when I arrived on the scene so that made it a bit easier, but it took me a long time to gain their trust. The one thing I can say is that it was worth the effort.'

Lewis sighed when he heard the warmth in her voice. 'You really love them, don't you?'

'Yes, I do. They may not be my biological children but I care about them just as much as if they were.'

'I can tell that. They were very lucky to have you. I only hope I can be half as good a father to Kristy.'

'You *are* a good father! It's obvious how much you care about her. I can hear it in your voice whenever you speak to her.'

'Can you?'

He wasn't sure why that comment made him feel so uneasy. Perhaps it was the thought that she seemed able to read him better than most people could. In his former life—*pre-Kristy*—he'd made it a rule to keep his emotions under wraps. It had been a bone of contention with several girlfriends, in fact. They'd accused him of shutting them out, but it was how he'd preferred to live his life—without any complications.

Kristy's advent into his life had changed all that, and he was no longer capable of hiding his feelings to such an extent. Take what had happened recently, for example. Normally, he wouldn't have given any thought to the amount of work Helen was doing. He would have considered it to be none of his business. However, he couldn't do that now. He cared what she did, but he had to be sensible and accept that he didn't have the right to interfere when he had nothing to offer her.

It was a salutary thought and it made him see how dangerous it would be to get any more deeply involved with her. It was especially dangerous when he was feeling so emotional and it was high time he got himself back on track. He stood up and reached for the coffee-pot.

'Shall I make some more coffee?' he asked with a deliberate lack of enthusiasm. Just a short while ago he'd been eager for her to stay but now he was just as eager for her to leave. It was only tempting fate to have her in his home and it was the last thing he should do when finally he'd made some progress with his daughter.

'Not for me, thanks. It really is time I went home.' Helen smiled politely as she stood up, but he could tell that she knew he wanted her to leave.

'At least it's Saturday tomorrow so you'll have some time to yourself,' he replied, trying to ignore the pangs of guilt. He knew that he had to put Kristy's interests before everything else but it wasn't easy to send Helen away. If he'd made some headway that night towards forging a closer bond with his daughter, then he'd also managed to get that bit closer to Helen as well. It was difficult to deal with the thought that he might not get another chance.

'Unfortunately, I need to work on the latest budget cuts the trust is demanding so my weekend will be spent in the surgery.'

Lewis winced when he heard the challenge in her voice. She was daring him to say something but there was no way he could do so now. He had to stop worrying about Helen so he could concentrate on Kristy.

'There's always something that needs doing, isn't there?' he observed as he followed her along the hall.

'Indeed.' She gave him a cool little smile and held out her hand. 'Thanks again for supper. You and Kristy must have supper with me one night.'

'That would be great.'

He shook her hand, knowing that the invitation would never amount to anything. It had been the polite thing to do and she didn't expect him to take her up on the offer. He opened the door and waited while she got into her car. She beeped the horn then drove away without a backward glance.

Lewis went back inside and set about all the jobs that needed to be done, trying not to notice how empty the house felt. He'd lived on his own out of choice for years, yet despite the fact that his daughter was asleep upstairs he was suddenly overwhelmed by a feeling of loneliness. Having Helen in his home had given him a glimpse of how his life might be if he had someone like her to share it, but there was no point thinking along those lines when he had Kristy to consider. He wouldn't be sharing his life with Helen or any other woman in the foreseeable future.

CHAPTER SIX

'CAN you check how many patients there are booked in to see me this morning, Eve? I still haven't made much headway with this year's budget and I need to get it sorted out.'

Helen waited while the receptionist checked the appointment book. It was Monday morning and the weekend had been a complete waste of time. She'd spent all day Saturday and most of Sunday wrestling with the figures, but she hadn't achieved very much. Maybe it was because her mind had kept wandering, she mused, then quickly blanked out the thought. She didn't need any more distractions that day!

'I make it twenty-five.' Eve looked guilty as she finished totting up the list. 'There were a couple of calls this morning and I added them to your list because they said it was urgent.'

Helen bit back a sigh. The maximum number of patients everyone was supposed to see each morning was twenty, although she couldn't remember the last time her list had been that short. There was an antenatal clinic that afternoon so it looked as though she would have to work on the budget after evening surgery.

'I could try postponing some of the less urgent appointments,' Eve offered. 'Mrs Hill only wants a repeat prescription so she doesn't really need to see you. And I know that Jenny Prescot just has a cold because her mum told me that when she phoned up.'

'No. I'd better see everyone if they've made an appointment,' Helen told her. 'But can you not add anyone else to my list today? And tell Janet not to do so either.'

'Of course,' Eve agreed hurriedly as the phone started to ring.

Helen moved away from the desk, wondering if she could snatch a few minutes after the antenatal clinic finished. If there weren't too many mums booked in, she might be able to squeeze in some paperwork before evening surgery started...

'Oh, no! How awful! Yes, yes, of course I'll tell her. She's here now... Right. Yes. I understand.'

Helen turned round and hurried back to the desk when she heard what Eve was saying. She could tell it was bad news because the receptionist looked very shaken as she put down the phone.

'That was Mrs Humphreys from the junior school,' Eve explained tremulously. 'A lorry has crashed into the playground and several children have been hurt. She's phoned the emergency services but she needs help until the ambulances get there.'

'I'll get straight over there,' Helen told her immediately. She was just about to run back to her room to fetch her case when the door opened, and her heart sank when she saw that Lewis had arrived. He always took Kristy to school before he came into work and she could only pray that the little girl hadn't been involved in the accident.

She hurried straight over to him, knowing there was no easy way to break the news. 'There's been an accident at the school— a lorry has crashed into the playground.'

All the colour drained from his face. 'Are any of the children hurt?'

'Yes. But I don't know how many or who they are. I'm going over there to help.'

'I'm coming with you.'

He didn't wait for her to reply as he ran back out to the car park. Helen fetched her bag and followed him. He didn't say a word as she jumped into the car but she understood. He must be worried sick at the thought of Kristy being one of the injured children and the last thing he would feel like doing was talking.

It took them just a few minutes to reach the school. News of the accident had obviously spread because there were dozens of parents milling about. The police had arrived as well and they were cordoning off the area around the lorry. Helen could see that the cab was embedded in the wall that surrounded the playground. The trailer it had been pulling had sheared off and there was a crowd of people clustered around it. It looked as though there was someone trapped underneath so she came to a swift decision.

'You go and find Kristy while I check what's going on over there.'

'Fine.'

Lewis didn't waste any time as he raced towards the school. She saw him speak to one of the policemen before he disappeared into the playground. There was nothing she could do to help him so she hurried over to the trailer.

'Oh, am I glad to see you, Dr Daniels!' a woman exclaimed.

'Is there someone under there?' Helen asked, kneeling down so she could see beneath the trailer. Fortunately, the front end had become wedged on some of the rubble from the wall and had been partly raised off the ground otherwise the person underneath would have been crushed. She could just make out a pair of jeans-clad legs but it was impossible to tell if they belonged to a man or a woman.

'It's Lucy Maguire…you know, that young girl with the two little boys.'

'Lucy? But I didn't think her children were old enough to go to school,' Helen exclaimed.

'The oldest boy…Ben…has just started at the nursery.'

'Ben isn't under there as well, is he?' she said in dismay, peering under the lorry again.

'No, no! Lucy had already taken him into school. She was on her way home when the accident happened. One of the other mums had just been speaking to her and Lucy had told her that she'd left the other little mite with a neighbour.' The woman sighed. 'Thank heavens for small mercies is all I can say.'

Helen silently agreed. However, her main concern was to find out how badly injured Lucy was. She got up and walked around the lorry but there was no easier way to get to the girl. She would have to crawl underneath and just hope it was securely lodged on those stones.

Shrugging off her coat, she knelt down and slithered into the gap, trying to blot out the thought of what could happen if the trailer shifted. There was just enough room for her to crawl over to Lucy. The girl was lying on her front and there was blood trickling out of her ear. Helen knew it could be the result of a serious head trauma and that she needed to get her out of there as quickly as possible.

She hurriedly checked Lucy for any other signs of injury but she couldn't find anything. As for spinal damage, that was something she couldn't rule out. It meant that not only would they have to get Lucy out as quickly as possible, but they would need to do so in a way which wouldn't exacerbate any existing injury. As she crawled out from under the trailer, she realised how difficult it was going to be.

'How is she?'

She looked up in surprise when she heard Lewis's voice. 'You were quick. Is Kristy all right?'

'She's fine. She was in the classroom when the accident happened.'

'That's great!' she declared, then suddenly sobered. 'What about the other children? Do you know how many have been injured?'

'Just three, and they've only got a few minor cuts and bruises. I checked them over while I was there and they're going to be fine. One of the mums has a broken leg as well, but that's it.'

'And the driver?'

'Dead.' His tone was sombre. 'It looks as though he might have suffered a heart attack. It would explain why this happened, wouldn't it? The poor chap probably couldn't do anything to prevent it.'

'It sounds likely,' she agreed sadly. 'Still, it could have been a lot worse if most of the children hadn't been in school.'

'It certainly could.' He glanced at the trailer. 'What have we got here?'

'One of the mums is trapped underneath. It's Lucy Maguire, little Josh's mum—remember?'

'Of course I remember her. How is she?'

'It's difficult to tell how badly injured she is because there's very little room under there. She's bleeding from her ears, though, so I'm assuming she's suffered a head injury. I can't find any obvious signs of fractures to her limbs, but I can't rule out spinal damage.'

'Which means we're going to have to handle her with kid gloves.' He crouched down and peered under the trailer. 'Would it be possible to get a cervical collar on her? It would help if we could stabilise her neck before we tried to move her.'

'She's lying on her front and I honestly don't think it's possible. There isn't enough room to roll her over so we'd have to lift her head to fit a collar and we can't take that risk.'

'Then we need to ensure that she doesn't try to move. I take it that she's unconscious?'

'At the moment, yes.'

'Then we'd better sedate her before we do anything else.'

He stripped off his jacket and dropped it on the ground then removed his tie. Helen hastily averted her eyes as he undid the top button of his shirt. It wasn't as though she hadn't seen a man undressing before so why did she feel all tingly because Lewis had undone a single shirt button? It was impossible to answer that question so she decided to err on the side of caution and look the other way.

'Helen?'

Helen flushed when she heard the quizzical note in his voice. However, there was no way that she was prepared to explain why she'd been staring into space so she ignored it. 'You won't have much room to manoeuvre once you're under there,' she told him briskly, crouching down. 'And the worst bit is trying to get under the front axle—there's barely enough room to slither through the gap.'

'So long as I can get a needle into her. That's all I'm aiming for.'

His tone was bland so she couldn't blame it for the shiver that raced through her. When he crouched down beside her, she carefully moved out of his way so there'd be less risk of them touching. He shot her a wry look and her heartbeat quickened when she realised that he'd noticed what she'd done.

'You don't have to worry about getting muck all over me. I'll be in the same state as you after I've been under there. The things we do for fun, eh?'

He looked pointedly at her and she gasped when she realised that her once pristine blouse was filthy from crawling under the lorry. Lifting the hem of the blouse, she sniffed at the sticky gunk that was spattered all over its front and grimaced. 'Oh, that is so disgusting! What on earth is it?'

Lewis leant forward until his nose was no more than a scant inch away from her right breast. 'Essence of farm manure with just a *soupçon* of diesel…. That's a point—I wonder if the fuel tank has ruptured?'

Helen held herself rigid. Even if she tried to back away, there was always a chance that his face and her breast would come into contact. 'I didn't notice any diesel leaking from it,' she said in a tight little voice.

'Maybe it didn't come from the lorry, then. It could be a patch of oil that's been spilt on the road at some time.' He straightened abruptly and she saw a rim of colour run along his cheekbones. 'I'll try to avoid it.'

With that, he slid under the trailer, inching his way forward until only his feet were visible. Helen bit her lip as a dozen emotions hit her all at once. Dealing with this awareness she felt whenever he was around was one thing. However, knowing that he was just as aware of her was something entirely different.

Her own sexuality was something she'd thought very little about in the past twelve years. Once she'd married Ian, her role in life had been secure, but she was no longer that person now. She was a woman in her own right, who—she'd discovered—had needs that couldn't be satisfied by her work. She wanted more than just her job, so much more that her head started buzzing as the enormity of what she wanted hit her.

She wanted to be thought of as a woman again.

She wanted to find out if those bells and whistles she'd dreamed about once upon a time were only to be found in fiction.

She also yearned for a child of her own, although maybe that was a dream too far, one which would always elude her. However, the fact that she had admitted her deepest longings showed how much she had changed, and it was all because of Lewis. He'd made her confront her feelings instead of burying them, as she had been doing. It scared her to know how great an influence he had on her.

'I think I can manage to give her the shot if you could pass it to me once I'm in position.'

Lewis was trying his best to behave as though nothing had happened but he couldn't believe how stupid he'd been. Bending down to sniff Helen's blouse had been an act of madness! His blood heated as he recalled how his face had been poised above her breast and he groaned. That memory was going to haunt him for many nights to come!

'Are you sure you don't want me to do it?'

'No, it's OK.' He blanked out the thought and made himself focus on what needed to be done. 'My arms are longer than yours so it will be easier for me to reach her.'

'Fine.'

Helen didn't argue as she drew up a shot of morphine and he breathed a sigh of relief. From this point on he would be far more careful what he did. 'I'm going back under there while you sort that out. I'll need to cut through her clothing before I can give it to her so I may as well get it done now.'

He took a pair of scissors out of his case and crawled under the lorry again, wincing when he felt something sticking into his ribs. There was a lot of debris about and it wasn't easy to find a clear route to get to Lucy. He'd almost reached her when her eyes suddenly opened, so he hurriedly stretched out his arm and grasped her hand.

'Lie still! It's absolutely vital that you don't try to move.'

'What's happened? Where am I?'

She attempted to turn her head and he quickly placed his free hand on the back of her neck to stop her moving. 'You've been in an accident, Lucy, and you need to keep very, very still.'

'An accident?' she repeated uncertainly.

Lewis inched himself forward until he was in a better position to control the situation if she started to panic. 'A lorry ran off the road and knocked you over. You're trapped under the trailer. The fire brigade is on its way and they'll soon get you out. In the meantime, I'm going to give you an injection—'

'No! I don't want any injections. I hate needles!'

There was real terror in her voice now and he frowned. The last thing he wanted was for her to get so agitated. Until they knew for certain whether she'd damaged her spine, they had to take every precaution possible.

'Then you have to lie completely still. You don't appear to have fractured anything but we can't tell if you've injured your spine. Any sudden movement could put you in extreme danger.'

'You mean I might not be able to walk again?'

'It's just a precaution to prevent that happening,' he assured her.

'Why did it have to happen to me?' Tears began to pour down her face and he squeezed her hand.

'You were in the wrong place at the wrong time. That's all.' He swivelled sideways when he heard Helen calling him. She was kneeling on the ground and he could tell that she wanted to speak to him. He turned to Lucy again, making his tone as sooth-ing as possible. 'I just need to speak to Dr Daniels…'

'You can't leave me here on my own!'

There was genuine panic in the young woman's voice and he realised that he didn't dare abandon her if they were to avert a disaster. 'I'm not going to leave you. I'll just have to move back a bit so I can speak to Dr Daniels, but I'll keep hold of your hand.'

He shuffled backwards until just their fingertips were touch-ing. It wasn't the easiest position in which to hold a conversa-tion but there was nothing he could do about it. Helen was lying flat on the ground now and he grimaced when he saw the ques-tion in her eyes.

'She's terrified of needles apparently,' he said softly, so Lucy couldn't hear him. 'She's refused to let me give her an injection.'

'Oh, I should have warned you!' Helen exclaimed in dismay. 'I know she hates needles but I didn't realise she'd regained consciousness.'

'It isn't your fault. It's just one of those things. Anyway, the best thing I can do is to stay with her until the fire crew gets here.'

'That's what I wanted to tell you. They've just arrived and they're assessing the situation.' She broke off and scrambled to her feet. When she reappeared there was a fireman with her. 'This is Station Officer Hammond. He's in charge of the accident scene.'

'Pleased to meet you,' Lewis replied honestly. 'How long will it take your men to get this trailer shifted?'

'We're getting everything set up but it will be a good thirty minutes before we can move it,' Officer Hammond explained. 'Dr Daniels tells me that the young woman might have a head injury.'

'That's right, so the sooner we get her out of here the better.' He didn't elaborate on the seriousness of the situation: Officer Hammond must have dealt with enough incidents to know that time was of the essence.

'We'll be as quick as we can. In the meantime, I'm going to send one of my guys to relieve you—'

'No way! I'm not leaving her. I promised her that I'd stay and that's what I intend to do.'

'Fair enough, but you do realise the danger you're putting yourself in, Doctor?'

'It's no worse for me than it would be for your men,' he pointed out. He glanced at Helen and smiled when he saw the worry in her eyes. 'Anyway, I wouldn't like to subject you lot to the aroma under here. You certainly won't thank me if you come out smelling of the manure the roses grew in!'

'Pass!' Officer Hammond said with a laugh, standing up.

'Are you sure you'll be all right?' Helen asked anxiously after the fireman had left.

'I'll be fine. Don't worry about me.'

Lewis didn't say anything else as he inched his way back under the trailer. He wasn't prepared to break his promise to Lucy and that was the end of the matter. However, he had to admit that it was good to know that Helen was concerned about him.

He tried to put that thought out of his mind as he went back to Lucy. 'The fire brigade has arrived so it shouldn't be too long now before they get you out.'

'That's good,' she mumbled.

Lewis felt a jolt of alarm run through him when he saw her eyes start to close. In the short time he'd been talking to Helen, Lucy's condition had deteriorated. He squeezed her hand, wanting to stop her losing consciousness. 'Were you taking your children to school when the accident happened?'

'I'd just…taken Ben to…nursery…' she said haltingly.

Lewis gripped her hand a bit harder. 'My little girl has just started attending this school. She's in Mrs Moore's class.'

'Used to be my teacher,' Lucy muttered, her voice slurring.

'Really? It must be great to be able to send your children to the same school that you went to.'

He was making conversation purely to try and keep her alert but there was no response this time. Letting go of her hand, he quickly crawled out from beneath the trailer. Helen was standing beside the lorry and he could see the alarm on her face when he appeared.

'Lucy's unconscious again. Her condition is deteriorating and we need to get her out of there immediately.'

'The fire crew is setting up some sort of lifting device,' she explained, pointing to where a group of firemen were working.

Lewis frowned when he saw what they were doing. 'It looks like they're going to use airbags to lift the front of the trailer. It will take some time to inflate them and I don't know if we can wait much longer.'

'They're doing all they can. Officer Hammond knows how urgent the situation is. I'm sure he'll get things moving as quickly as possible.'

'You're right, of course. It's just so frustrating, not being able to do more to help her.'

'I know, but we can only do our best, Lewis. We can't work miracles.'

'Sadly not.' He summoned a smile, knowing it was pointless labouring the point. Helen was right—everything possible was being done and he had to be patient. The ambulances had arrived now and he shook his head when one of the paramedics offered to take over from him. 'I'd rather see this through to the end. Thanks.'

'Are you sure?' she said quickly. 'You don't have to do this, Lewis. The paramedics are used to dealing with this type of situation.'

'I know that, but I can't just abandon Lucy. I promised her that I'd stay with her and that's what I'll do.'

Helen's eyes filled with warmth. 'Then of course you must stay.'

'Are you going to hang on here, or are you going back to the surgery now that reinforcements have arrived?' he asked softly. Maybe it was silly to read too much into the way she was looking at him but he couldn't help it. His heart seemed to swell to double its normal size when she smiled at him.

'Of course I'm staying! I don't intend to leave until I know you're all right…you and Lucy, I mean.'

A little colour touched her cheeks as she turned away, but he'd already seen it. As he crawled back under the trailer, he could feel his heart pounding. Helen had tried to cover up her slip but she wasn't an accomplished liar. The reason she was staying was because of him and he couldn't explain how good it felt to know that she cared. In some strange way it helped make up for all the lonely days and nights he'd spent this past year, worrying about Kristy.

Helen's nerves were stretched to breaking point by the time the fire crew finally managed to raise the trailer enough to get Lucy out. Lewis had steadfastly refused to leave her even though he'd been warned several times about the danger he was in. True to his word, he'd stayed with Lucy the entire time and Helen was filled with admiration for his bravery.

'She's been bleeding from the ears so she's going to need a CT scan as soon as you get her to hospital. She regained consciousness at one point but her condition deteriorated so it looks as though she's suffered a serious head injury.'

Lewis accompanied the paramedics to the ambulance while he continued updating them, and Helen went with him. They had moved Lucy onto a spinal board as soon as they'd been able to get at her. The paramedics had fitted her with a cervical collar and also used a padded head restraint to further minimise any risk of movement during the journey. One of the crew was now setting up a drip—essential to prevent Lucy lapsing into shock if she was bleeding internally. Helen knew that everything possible was being done for her but there was no guarantee that she would pull through.

'Don't worry, Doc, you can leave her to us now,' one of the paramedics told him. 'We'll take good care of her.'

Helen glanced at Lewis as the ambulance drove away. 'That's it, then. We did everything we could and we'll just have to see what happens.'

'I just hope she makes it.' He sighed as he ran a grimy hand over his face. 'It's a crying shame when you think about those two little boys.'

'I don't know what's going to happen to the children while Lucy is in hospital. Her partner walked out on her last year and she's been on her own since then.'

'Does she have any family in the town?' he asked as they walked back to the car.

'Not that I'm aware of. Janet or Eve might know but I've never heard Lucy mention any family. I got the impression that she was on her own.'

'Maybe we should contact Social Services and see if they can help,' he suggested, stopping beside the car. 'Even if she pulls through, she's going to be in hospital for some time so someone is going to have to take care of those children.'

'I'll get in touch with the duty social worker as soon as we get back to the surgery.' She sighed sadly. 'It must be your worst nightmare when you're a single parent. Worrying what will happen to the children if you're taken ill must be very difficult.'

'It is.' His tone was sombre. 'If anything happens to me, Kristy will be on her own.'

'Sorry. I didn't mean to touch a nerve.'

'You only highlighted something I've thought about before.'

'Maybe.' She gave a little shrug, hating to think that she might have upset him. 'Anyway, what are you going to do now? I imagine you want to check on Kristy, don't you?'

'Yes. The headmistress might decide to send the children home now that they've cleared the playground.' He glanced at his watch and groaned. 'Is that the time? Heaven knows how Harry is coping at the surgery.'

'He's probably been run off his feet. Look, why don't I head back there while you sort out the arrangements for Kristy? Just let me know if you need to take the rest of the day off, will you?'

Lewis shook his head. 'There's no way I'm leaving you in the lurch. If push comes to shove, I'll bring her into work, so long as you don't mind?'

'Of course I don't mind! You do whatever you think is best and we'll take it from there.'

'Thanks.'

He gave her a quick smile then hurried away. Helen didn't waste any time as she made her way home to get changed. Fortunately, it was only a five minute walk from the school to her house but it was gone eleven by the time she made it back to the surgery. Her heart sank when she went into the waiting-room and saw all the people sitting there. There was a huge back-log and she could understand why Eve and Janet greeted her with such relief.

'Looks as though it's been a tad hectic in here,' she observed drolly as she went into the office.

'You can say that again!' Janet rolled her eyes. 'Poor Harry has done his best but he's been absolutely swamped.'

'The sooner I get down to some work the better, then.' Helen turned to go then paused when Eve came hurrying through from Reception.

'How's Lucy? One of the mums told us that she was trapped under the lorry.'

'She's been taken to hospital with a suspected head injury,' she explained. 'That's all I can tell you for now. I'll give the hospital a call after lunch when they might have some more news.'

'Oh, the poor thing! I do hope she'll be all right. What's going to happen to those two little kiddies of hers?' Janet asked worriedly.

'I don't know,' Helen admitted. 'Does Lucy have any family living in the area who could look after them? She's never mentioned anyone to me but maybe she has relatives near by.'

'Her parents died when she was a child,' Janet explained sadly. 'Her grandparents brought her up but they passed away some years ago. That's when Lucy moved away. She went to live in London and only came back last year after she'd split up with the boys' father.'

'Then I'd better have a word with Social Services and see what they can suggest. Can you get the duty social worker on the phone for me? I may as well sort this out before I do anything else.'

Helen went to her room. Janet soon found the number she needed so she told the social worker what had happened and was assured that they would handle things from there on. After that it was a case of trying to catch up.

The morning flew past and it was lunchtime before she knew it. She gathered together the files she'd used after her last patient had left and took them back to the office. Lewis was coming along the corridor when she left her room so she stopped to wait for him.

'How did you get on at school? Did you have to take Kristy home?'

'No. The head decided it would cause too many problems if she sent the children home. A lot of parents had gone to work when the accident happened so she couldn't be sure of getting in contact with them. She spoke to the police and the fire brigade and they assured her there was no danger so she decided to carry on as normal.' He shrugged. 'Any parents who wanted to take their child home could do so, but I decided it would be less disruptive for Kristy if she stuck to her normal routine.'

'And what about tonight? Are they still holding the after-school club?'

'Apparently.' He opened the office door then stepped back so she could precede him.

'Thanks.' Helen went to enter the room, pausing when she heard his swift intake of breath as she accidentally brushed against him. She looked at him in concern when she saw how pale he'd gone. 'Are you all right?'

'I'm fine. I managed to cut myself on some broken glass when I was under that lorry. I've put a dressing on it but it's still a bit tender.'

'Do you want me to take a look at it for you?' she offered, dropping her files into the tray.

'No, it's OK.' He shrugged as he added his bundle to hers. 'It's just a cut and it will soon heal.'

'How long is it since you had a tetanus jab?' she persisted.

'I've no idea.' He grimaced. 'I know what you're going to say—everyone should have a booster every few years. I just never seem to get round to it.'

'Then there's no time like the present, is there?' She went to the door, arching her brows when he didn't make any attempt to follow her. 'Well, what are you waiting for? Surely you're not frightened of needles?'

'No, although I can think of more pleasant ways to spend my lunch-break.' He chuckled as he followed her out of the office. 'Are you always this bossy?'

'Only when I need to be,' she replied loftily, leading the way to the treatment room. They kept a stock of vaccines on hand so she took a vial of the tetanus booster out of the cabinet, placed it in a dish then found a syringe. 'I'd like to check the cut before I give you the shot, though. It's not easy to clean a wound properly yourself and there's no point taking any chances.'

'There really isn't any need.' He sighed when she didn't reply. 'Oh, all right. If you insist.'

He unbuttoned his shirt and turned so that she could see the dressing on the right side of his ribs. Helen took a pair of gloves out of the box and put them on before carefully removing the lint. She frowned when she saw the jagged cut that had scored his flesh.

'It's quite deep. '

'There was a lot of debris under that trailer.'

'There was also a lot of muck under there so I'll clean it up again to make sure there's no dirt in it. Just stay there while I fetch what I need.'

She quickly gathered together some antiseptic and cotton wool then set to work, cleaning the cut and the area surrounding it with antiseptic solution. She was so engrossed that it was only when she reached for a fresh piece of cotton wool that she noticed the strained expression on his face.

'Sorry. Did that hurt?'

'No, it's fine.' His voice sounded unusually gruff despite the reassurance, and she hesitated.

'Are you sure? If it's that painful maybe there's a fragment of glass in it. I'd better check to make sure.'

She turned away to fetch the magnifying glass they kept for just such an occasion then paused when he said softly behind her, 'It's not the cut, Helen.'

There was something in his voice that made her heart suddenly pound. She could feel it thumping away as she turned to face him. 'If it's not the cut, what is it?' she asked in a voice that sounded unlike her normal tone.

'I think you know what it is.'

He took a slow step towards her and a shiver danced down her spine when she saw the way he was looking at her. She couldn't remember a man looking at her before with such desire in his eyes, not even Ian.

The thought stunned her so that she could only stand there as though she'd been rooted to the spot as he took another step which brought him within touching distance this time.

'It's you, Helen…and how you make me feel.'

CHAPTER SEVEN

'LEWIS, I....' Helen stopped when there was a sudden knock on the door. She just had time to step back before Janet appeared.

'Sorry to bother you, Helen, but the social worker is here to see you about Lucy Maguire,' the receptionist explained, looking startled when she saw Lewis's state of undress.

'Thank you, Janet. Can you show her into my office?'

Helen made a determined effort to collect herself but her heart was beating almost out of control. She didn't dare speculate what might have happened if they hadn't been interrupted. She summoned a smile because the last thing she wanted was for there to be any gossip in the surgery. 'Lewis managed to cut himself while he was helping Lucy this morning. I was just cleaning the wound for him.'

'Oh, how awful!' Janet exclaimed in concern. 'Amy's in the staffroom so shall I ask her to see to it while you deal with the social worker?'

'That would be a big help.' Helen peeled off her gloves and dropped them into the bin. Maybe she couldn't say for certain what would have happened, but she could make an educated guess!

Her cheeks flamed at the thought of what the receptionist might have witnessed. Seeing her and Lewis kissing certainly wasn't the kind of behaviour the staff would expect to see. In the whole time she and Ian had been married they had never once kissed each other while they'd been at work. Ian had had set views on such matters and would have considered it highly unprofessional behaviour, and she had respected him for it. However, just a couple of weeks after meeting Lewis, all her principles seemed to have gone by the board.

It was painful to realise that she had let herself down. She turned to Lewis as the receptionist hurried away, wanting to make it clear that there would never be a repeat of what had happened that day. 'Amy can give you the tetanus shot. Make sure you ask her for it, won't you?'

'Of course.'

His tone was every bit as distant as hers had been so she couldn't understand why it upset her so much. As she left the treatment room, she told herself it was silly to let it bother her. Maybe Lewis had realised the mistake they'd nearly made and regretted it, as she did. Only that thought didn't make her feel any better.

She sighed. Two wrongs definitely didn't make this situation feel right.

What the hell had he been thinking?

Lewis could barely contain his frustration as he made his way back to his room a short time later. He knew that he'd made a major blunder with Helen and knew, too, that there was little chance of him putting things right. He only had to recall the expression on her face as she'd left the room to know that he wouldn't get a chance to explain himself.

He groaned as he sat down at his desk. What kind of explanation could he have given her? That he'd been so overcome by desire that he'd wanted to make mad, passionate love to her? He could just imagine her response if he told her that! She would probably terminate his contract and he'd find himself out of a job...

Or would he?

Why should he assume that she would have reacted that way? She'd had plenty of time to tell him to stop but she hadn't made any attempt to do so. She'd just stood there and there was no point pretending that he hadn't seen the desire in her eyes, because he had!

The truth was that she hadn't wanted him to stop. She'd wanted him to take her in his arms and make love to her right there in the surgery. For once in her life she had reacted with her heart, not her head, and in her heart she'd wanted him. She had!

Lewis shot to his feet. He knew that he needed to sort out the situation as quickly as possible. If he waited then Helen would find a way to rationalise what had happened and he didn't want her doing that...did he?

His head spun as one side of his brain argued with the other, leaving him in the middle to referee. He wanted to make Helen admit that she'd desired him, yet he was afraid of what it could lead to. Once he'd uncovered the truth, it couldn't be hidden away again. He would have to act on it, and he wasn't in a position to do that.

The fact was that he couldn't have a relationship with anyone when he had Kristy to consider. And Helen wasn't just anyone. She was someone special, so special that she had the power to destroy all the plans he'd made for being a good father. How could he take that risk? How could he be so selfish as to put his own happiness above that of his daughter?

He sank down on the chair again. He couldn't involve Helen in his life, now or in the future.

The day was one of the busiest Helen could remember, but at least it meant she had less time to brood about what had happened. After the social worker left, she got ready for the antenatal clinic. The clinic was her favourite part of the week. Watching a new life develop was a real joy and she took extra care as she discussed any problems the mums-to-be had. She wanted them to enjoy their pregnancies, although not everyone felt it a reason for celebration.

Lisa Pendleton fell into that category and every time she visited the surgery Helen had to make a special effort not to be sharp with her. It was harder than ever that day when presented with the young woman's litany of complaints.

'I feel like such a freak! I can't wear anything decent because of this bump!'

Lisa stepped off the scales and glared down at her expanding waistline. She'd reached the twenty-week mark and her tummy was getting quite large. Helen murmured a few soothing noises as she made a note of Lisa's weight, but it wasn't enough to satisfy the young woman.

'I wish I hadn't gone ahead and had the baby now. I was going to have a termination but Aidan talked me out of it.' Lisa glowered as she put on her shoes. 'I shouldn't have listened to him. I mean, it's not *him* who's having to go through all this!'

'A lot of women get upset when they see their bodies changing,' Helen assured her. 'But once you've had your baby, you'll soon be back to your old self.'

'My sister isn't. She *piled* on weight when she had her little boy and she's never lost it. Ryan's two next week and she still looks as though she's pregnant!' Lisa plonked herself down on a chair. 'I don't see why my life should be ruined because of some kid. Maybe it's not too late to get rid of it.'

'That would be a very drastic step, Lisa,' Helen said firmly, trying not to let the girl see how appalled she was by the idea. 'Your hormones run riot when you're pregnant and I expect that's why you're feeling so down at the moment.'

'It's not my hormones. I've been thinking about what I'm going to do after the baby's born. OK, so Aidan swears that he's going to help me look after it but I know what he's like.' Lisa tossed her head. 'He'll be down the pub with his mates while I'm stuck at home with a screaming brat, and I'm just not prepared to put up with it, Dr Daniels.'

'Looking after a new baby isn't easy, Lisa, and I won't try to tell you that it is. However, I'm sure you will cope perfectly well once he or she is born.'

Helen chose her words with care, wishing that she didn't

have to face this dilemma today of all days. Her feelings were already very raw, thanks to what had happened earlier, and it wasn't easy to behave in a professional manner when faced with such an emotive subject. The fact that Lisa could think of aborting her child at this stage was truly horrifying, but she was bound by professional ethics not to say that to her.

'How do you know that I'll cope?' Lisa retorted. 'I've never had anything to do with kids—never wanted to either.'

'Because you'll learn as you go along. I knew very little about being a parent but I learned what to do as the twins grew up. In a way, I grew up with them. What I do know is that I wouldn't have missed those years for anything.'

'Ah, but it was different for you, Dr Daniels. The twins aren't your real children so you didn't have to go through the hassle of actually giving birth to them.' Lisa stared balefully at her bump. 'You also didn't have to sit around wondering if you were going to spend the rest of your life looking like a beached whale.'

'No, I didn't give birth to Tom and Katie, although I wish I had. I would love to have experienced all the highs and the lows of childbirth.'

Helen tried not to let her emotions surface but the comment had touched a nerve. If Ian hadn't been so determined not to add to his family, she might have been able to speak from experience. However, his selfishness had denied her the thing she'd wanted more than anything else: a baby of her own.

The thought shocked her to the core. She couldn't believe that she'd just thought of Ian as selfish. Ian had been a kind and gentle man, and she was appalled that she should have denigrated his memory that way. She stood up, needing to bring the discussion to an end before anything else happened, but Lisa obviously still had issues to resolve.

'What's the cut-off point for having a termination?'

'Under current UK law it's twenty-four weeks,' Helen explained hollowly. 'However, you can't just have a termination on demand, Lisa. Unless it's a medical emergency and the mother's life is in danger, two doctors have to assess a woman's situation and there are strict guidelines that have to be followed.

'Abortion may only be performed if continuing the pregnancy would present a risk to the mother's life, or if there's a risk to the mental or physical health of the woman or her existing children. It's also permitted if there is substantial risk of serious handicap to the baby, although there is no question of that in your case. Your baby is perfectly healthy.'

'But there's still time for me to have a termination?' Lisa insisted.

'In theory, yes. However, each case has to be assessed on its own merits.' Helen took a deep breath but she simply couldn't hold back any longer. 'Quite frankly, Lisa, I think you'd be wrong to have a termination. You have a healthy child developing inside you. Maybe it isn't the most wonderful experience of your life but you could regret it if you decide to abort the baby.'

'That's just your opinion. And as I said before, you have no idea how I feel because you've not been in my position.' Lisa stood up and glared at her. 'I don't need you preaching at me, Dr Daniels, thank you very much!'

She stormed out of the room, leaving Helen with the sinking feeling that she'd made a mess of things. She should have tried harder to understand what Lisa was going through, and been more supportive. If she hadn't been so emotionally keyed up she would have handled the situation better and it was distressing to know that she'd allowed her personal feelings to get in the way of doing her job.

As she went to call in the next mum, she vowed it wouldn't happen again. No matter how stressful she found working with Lewis, she would keep a tight rein on herself in future. It shouldn't be that difficult because there wasn't going to be a repeat of what had happened that lunchtime. She intended to learn by her mistakes, not repeat them.

It was gone four by the time Lewis got back from doing the house calls and evening surgery had started. It had been a long list that day and he'd been late setting off, but what had delayed him most had been his car. As he let himself into the surgery, he realised that he was going to have to change the car as soon as possible.

'Sorry I'm late. I got caught out at one of the farms. I couldn't get down the road in my car so I had to leave it at the top and walk the rest of the way,' he explained as he hurried into the office.

'Well, if you will drive those posh vehicles, what do you expect?' Janet teased, and he groaned.

'Not so posh if it can't do the job it's supposed to do. Sports cars and farmyards definitely don't mix so it will have to go. Where's the best place around here to buy a new car?'

'Jack Thomson has a showroom in town, which is where most folk go—although I don't know if he'll have anything to interest you,' Janet added dubiously.

'So long as it has four wheels big enough to clamber over the ruts, it will be fine,' he assured her, grinning. He grabbed the pile of files stacked in his tray and headed for the door. 'Just give me a couple of minutes to get sorted out then you can send in my first customer.'

He hurried along the corridor to his room. Harry's door was shut so obviously he had a patient with him, and Helen's door was also closed, although maybe she'd shut it when she'd heard him coming in. He wouldn't blame her if she had because he could understand why she wouldn't want to speak to him.

He sighed as he tossed the files onto his desk. All afternoon long he'd thought about what had happened. He knew it would be wrong to involve Helen in his life but it didn't mean that he didn't want to. The thought of having her there whenever he needed someone to turn to was very appealing, but it wouldn't be fair if he started an affair with her…

He shook his head when he realised how arrogant it was of him to assume that she would be interested in having an affair with him. Maybe she hadn't exactly run screaming from the room at lunchtime but it would be silly to make that assumption.

She was a normal, healthy woman who had needs the same as any other woman, but it didn't mean that she wanted *him* in particular. Her response could have been the very natural result of two years of celibacy.

The thought was rather deflating and he wasn't sorry to put it out of his mind when his first patient arrived. He didn't need a battered ego to add to his woes!

Helen saw her final patient out then set to work on the budget. She felt tired and stressed, and the thought of a long soak in a hot bath was very tempting, but she was responsible for running the practice and she couldn't go home when there was work that needed doing. She would get it finished tonight even if she had to chain herself to her desk!

The trust had demanded quite a large reduction to their drugs bill and she couldn't seem to find a way to make the necessary cuts. She was just totting up the figures for the third time when Harry popped his head round the door.

'I thought you must be here when I saw your light was on. What's up?'

'Budget cuts,' Helen explained succinctly, keying another row of numbers into her calculator.

'Need a hand?' Harry offered.

'Thanks, but it's down to me to get it done.' She treated him to an abstracted smile. Obviously something had gone wrong because the total on the calculator's display was far larger than it should have been.

'Well, if you're sure...?'

'I am. Thanks, though, Harry. I appreciate the offer.'

Helen picked up her pen after the locum had left. Maybe it would work better if she resorted to the old-fashioned method of pen and paper? She wrote down the figures then added them up in her head but the answer came out the same. She'd made a mistake somewhere and now the trick was to find it. She sighed. It looked as though it was going to be a very long night indeed.

* * *

Lewis wasn't sure what made him drive past the surgery on his way back from picking up Kristy from the after-school club. It wasn't his usual route but for some reason he turned left instead of right at the roundabout. He slowed as he approached the surgery and realised that the lights were still on. It was half past six and he couldn't understand why the place was lit up...unless Helen was still in there, working.

His mouth thinned as he drove home because there was very little he could do about it. If she chose to extend her working day, that was her business. However, he couldn't shake off the image of her slaving away at her desk. Couldn't she see that she was in danger of burning herself out? And for what? To uphold her late husband's exacting standards?

Kristy was rather subdued when they got home. He suspected that the incident with the lorry had affected her and he hoped it wouldn't unsettle her too much. She'd been far less withdrawn since he'd suggested those riding lessons and he would hate to think that she'd taken a backward step.

He realised that he still hadn't got the riding instructor's phone number from Helen, and that he must do so soon. He wouldn't want Kristy to think that he didn't keep his promises so maybe he should get it from her tonight? It would give Kristy a boost to know when she would be starting her lessons so he would pop back to the surgery and ask Helen for it. And while he was there, maybe he should offer to help? She might appreciate an extra pair of hands, plus it would be a good way to put things back on a level footing. If he made it clear that he was only interested in having a professional relationship with her, it would make the situation easier for both of them.

He told Kristy they would be going out after tea. She seemed a bit uncertain at first because it wasn't usual for them to go out on a school night. However, she immediately brightened when he explained that he wanted to ask Helen for the phone number of the riding school. He also explained that he might want to help Helen do some work, and Kristy seemed quite amenable to the idea.

The surgery lights were still on when he drew up in the car park so he helped Kristy out of the car then used his key to let them in. Holding her hand, he headed along the corridor and stopped outside Helen's door, feeling his heart pounding. Once he knocked on the door, there would be no going back so was he absolutely certain about what he was doing? In other words, was he here purely because he wanted to keep his promise to his daughter and help a colleague? Or was he here because he wanted to see Helen? All of a sudden he was no longer sure about his motives.

CHAPTER EIGHT

'HELEN!'

Lewis jumped when Kristy suddenly shouted Helen's name. Before he could do anything, she knocked on the door. He knew his face must be a picture when a moment later Helen appeared.

'Hello! What are you doing here?'

Helen ignored him as she bent own and smiled at Kristy, and for some reason he felt more than a little put out. Maybe he wasn't exactly flavour of the month, but did she have to make it so obvious that she wasn't pleased to see him? All of a sudden he could see how stupid he'd been to imagine that she might welcome his help. She didn't want anything to do with him so he would just ask her for the phone number and leave.

'I'm sorry to disturb you but can you let me have that phone number for the riding instructor?' He shrugged when she glanced up. 'I might be able to arrange a lesson this weekend if I phone her tonight.'

'Of course. I should have given it to you before.'

She went back into the room and opened the top drawer of her desk. Lewis frowned when saw the stack of papers that were piled on top of it. 'Looks as though you've been busy.'

'It's that wretched budget. I can't seem to get the figures to add up... Ah, here it is.' She took an address book out of the drawer and jotted the number down on a scrap of paper then handed it to him. 'Tell Jill that I recommended you. She doesn't take many pupils because she's so busy with her own family, but I'm sure she will squeeze Kristy in.'

'Thanks. I will.' Lewis tucked the paper into his pocket then glanced at the desk. 'Have you got much more to do?'

'In theory, no.' She frowned as she picked up one of the sheets. 'All I need to do now is sort out the drugs bill. The problem is that the figures don't make sense. The total is way higher than it should be.'

'You must have made an error somewhere,' he said lightly, and she grimaced.

'I know! But it's finding it that's causing the problem.' She gave a little shrug. 'Not to worry. I'll get there in the end.'

'I'm sure you will.' He summoned a smile because it was obvious that she wasn't going to ask him for help. 'We'd better leave you to it, then…'

'Daddy said he was going to help you,' Kristy suddenly announced. She beamed up at him. 'That's right, isn't it, Daddy?'

'I…um… Yes.' Lewis knew he'd been caught red-handed and that there was no point lying. Anyway, it wouldn't set a good example for Kristy if she heard him telling an untruth. He squared his shoulders and looked Helen in the eye. 'I had this crazy idea that you might be glad of some help but I can see now that I was wrong so we'll get out of your way.'

He took hold of Kristy's hand and turned to leave, then paused when Helen said quickly, 'Wait!'

He glanced round, feeling his senses swim when he saw the expression on her face. He couldn't recall seeing such a mix of emotions on anyone's face before. She was just as confused by her feelings as he was, he realised. And it was painful to know that he was causing her all this distress.

'I'm sorry, Helen. I shouldn't have come. It was a silly thing to do in the circumstances.'

'It wasn't silly. It was very…kind.' She stumbled over the word and hurried on. 'I hate doing paperwork, especially budgets. Maths was never my best subject.'

'Or mine,' he said, forcing a smile. The fact that she hadn't questioned what he'd meant by 'circumstances' told him just how aware she was of the situation. It took a supreme effort to continue when he knew how dangerous it was. 'However, on the principle of two heads being better than one, I'm willing to give it a shot if you are.'

'It's kind of you to offer, but what about Kristy?' She smiled at the little girl. 'We don't want you getting bored while we're doing all these horrible sums, do we?'

'Maybe Kristy could draw while we're working?' He turned to his daughter, using the small breathing space to get himself back onto some sort of even emotional level. 'You don't mind drawing some pictures while Helen and I work, do you, darling?'

'Drawing's boss,' the child replied authoritatively.

'*Boss?*' he repeated, his brows rising as he glanced at Helen.

'It sounds to me as though someone's been talking to Danny Appleton,' she said with a smile, taking a wad of clean paper off the desk.

'Danny's my best friend at school,' Kristy told them importantly.

'I thought so.' Helen gave her some coloured highlighter pens and got her settled on the couch then sat down at her desk. Lewis pulled up a chair and sat down beside her, intrigued to know how she'd worked out who his daughter had been talking to.

'How did you know about Danny Appleton? Kristy's never even mentioned him to me.'

'Aha! That would be telling, wouldn't it?'

'Don't be so mean!' He laughed when she tapped the side of her nose. 'I'm dying to know your secret. You don't work for MI5, do you?'

'No, I don't. It was a simple deduction, actually. Danny Appleton's parents are the only people I've heard use that expression. His family come from Liverpool and I believe it's widely used there.' She grinned at him. 'Sometimes it helps to have a bit of inside knowledge.'

'So I can see.' He shook his head. 'I'll need to have my wits about me if I hope to keep up.'

'I don't know about that. I might know a lot about the people in this town but it doesn't help when it comes to these figures. It's going to take more than inside knowledge to get this little lot sorted out.'

She shrugged off the compliment and he sighed under his breath. Obviously, she had drawn a demarcation line and wouldn't allow him to cross over it onto what she considered personal territory. He turned his attention to the figures, knowing it would be best to stick to her rules. Anyway, there was no point trying to foster a closer relationship when nothing could come of it.

They worked for over an hour but they still couldn't find the error. Each time they added up the figures, the total was several thousand pounds more than it should have been. Lewis groaned as he stared at the calculator.

'I don't know what's going on. We should have saved almost four thousand pounds so why do we keep getting the same answer all the time?'

'I don't know.' Helen looked dejected as she studied the columns of figures. 'I think my brain has turned to mush after the number of times we've added this up.'

'You need a breather,' he said firmly, standing up. 'How about a cup of coffee before we try again?'

'I'd love one but what about Kristy? Isn't it time she was in bed?'

Lewis grimaced as he checked his watch. 'I didn't realise it was so late.'

'It must be past her bedtime by now and it isn't fair to her to keep her here any longer.' She winced as she stood up and flexed her shoulders. 'Oh, I'm so stiff from poring over these rotten figures!'

'Here, let me give your shoulders a rub.' Lewis didn't stop to think about the wisdom of what he was doing as he stepped behind her. He ran his hands over the base of her neck until he found the spot where there was the most tension and gently kneaded it.

Helen groaned as she let her head fall forward. 'That feels so good.'

'Does it?' Using his thumbs, he worked the knot out of the muscles and heard her moan with pleasure. It was only a tiny sound yet it had a galvanising effect on him. All of a sudden he was overwhelmed by the feel of her skin under his fingertips. It felt so wonderfully soft and smooth that he couldn't help wondering if the skin all over her body would feel the same. His body responded in time-honoured fashion to the thought and he shifted uncomfortably to ease the growing tightness in his groin, and heard her sigh.

'Much as I'm enjoying this, you really must stop. Kristy needs to go home to bed and I need to get this wretched budget finished.'

Lewis hurriedly stepped back as she turned, willing his traitorous body to settle down. This was neither the time nor the place for such an exuberant response! 'You're right. She's usually asleep by now so I'd better take her home. What about you, though? You're not going to stay here much longer, are you?'

'I'll take the figures home and work on them there.' She shrugged when he looked at her in concern. 'I have to get it done tonight, Lewis. The trust is waiting for my report.'

'Then come home with me and we'll work on it together,' he said impulsively, because he couldn't bear to think of her burning the midnight oil on her own.

'Oh, no. I couldn't...'

'Of course you could!' he said with a firmness that seemed to stop her in her tracks.

'Are you sure? I mean, there's Kristy and...'

'Yes, I'm sure. It will only take half an hour to get Kristy ready for bed then we can spend the rest of the evening sorting out the figures. It's too much for you to do on your own, Helen, so I won't take no for an answer.'

'I would be glad of the help,' she conceded.

'Good.'

He had to stop himself punching the air in triumph. For Helen to admit that she needed help was the first step towards her admitting that she'd been working too hard. His heart soared at the thought, even though he wasn't sure why it meant so much to him. He decided not to complicate the issue by thinking about it right then and smiled at her.

'I'll get Kristy ready while you make sure that you have everything you need. One way or the other, that budget will be finished tonight!'

She laughed at that. 'I might hold you to that promise! I just wish there was a budget fairy who would do it for me. I absolutely dread this time of the year because I know I'll have to spend *days* wrestling with the figures.'

'Have you never thought about hiring a practice manager?' he suggested as he helped Kristy gather up all her drawings.

'Not really. Ian preferred to do everything himself. He would never have thought of hiring someone to take care of the paperwork.'

'I understand that, but you don't have to do the same thing, do you, Helen?' He chose his words with care. The last thing he wanted was to upset her by riding roughshod over her feelings for her late husband. The thought that she might still be in love with her husband sent a pang coursing through him and he hurried on. 'You're in charge of the practice now and you can make any changes you want to.'

'I have thought about it,' she admitted. 'I just wasn't sure if it would be…well, *right*.'

Lewis knew that he mustn't push her. The fact that she'd admitted things might have to change was a step in the right direction and he must be satisfied with that. 'Only you can decide that, of course. However, a lot of practices employ a manager these days. The patients benefit as well as the staff because it frees up so much time that would have to be spent less productively otherwise.'

'It would be marvellous to have a bit more time each week,' she said wistfully.

'Then it might be worth considering.'

He didn't say anything else. There was always the danger that she might decide against the idea if he pushed her, and that was the last thing he wanted. Helen collected all her paperwork then they left the surgery together. He helped Kristy into his car while Helen set the alarm. The little girl was obviously tired because she started yawning while he was fastening her seat belt.

'We'll be home very soon, sweetheart,' he told her.

'Can Helen read me a story when I'm in bed?'

'We'll see.' He smiled at her then glanced round when he heard footsteps. 'Is that it, then?' he asked as Helen joined them. 'You've got everything you need?'

'I hope so. I certainly don't feel like coming back here again tonight.'

Lewis managed to hide his surprise, although it was the first time he'd ever heard her admit that she was tired of being in the surgery. 'Amen to that,' he replied lightly, not wanting to make an issue of it. 'I'll see you back at the house.'

'If you're sure you don't mind…?'

'I don't.'

He didn't give her time to change her mind as he got into the car. He stopped at the end of the drive to check the road was clear then pulled out. Glancing in the rear-view mirror, he saw Helen stop and held his breath. It still wasn't too late for her to reconsider…

She pulled out of the drive and followed him along the road, and he breathed a sigh of relief. So far so good! Now all he could hope was that the rest of the evening would go as smoothly. If he could help her work out those figures then he'd not only be doing her a favour but it would make him feel better, too. He couldn't bear to think of her working so hard all the time. She deserved so much more out of life. She deserved all the things a woman should have—a home and family, a man to love her…

He gripped the steering-wheel when he realised where the thought was leading, but there was no point lying to himself. If circumstances had been different, he would have applied for the role of Helen's partner in life as well as in work.

'Where's the best place to work?'

Helen took off her coat and draped it over the back of a kitchen chair. Now that they'd arrived at Lewis's home, she was starting to wonder if it had been a good idea. Admittedly, she would welcome his help with sorting out the budget, but was it really wise to do so in the intimacy of his home?

'How about if we stay in here?' He helped Kristy out of her coat and hung it on a peg. 'We need a table big enough to spread out all those papers and this is the biggest one in the house.'

'Fine by me,' she agreed, feeling a little easier at the thought of them working in the kitchen. There was something soothing about the idea of them sitting at the scrubbed-pine table that made her fears seem rather foolish. Opening her briefcase, she arranged the papers on the table then glanced up when Kristy came over to her.

'Will you read me a bedtime story, please?' the little girl asked shyly.

'Of course, I will, darling. So long as it's all right with your daddy, of course.' She glanced at Lewis for confirmation and he grinned at her.

'Of course it's all right with me! You don't need to ask. I'll get her ready then give you a shout when she's in bed, shall I?'

'Fine,' she agreed, trying not to let him see the effect that grin had had on her. She huffed out a sigh as he escorted Kristy from the room. She had to get a grip on herself otherwise she wouldn't be able to concentrate on the wretched figures. Acting like a love-struck teenager just because Lewis had smiled at her was absolutely ridiculous!

She found the calculator and tried adding the numbers up again but the answer was still more than it should have been. She had no idea where she'd gone wrong and only hoped that Lewis would be able to find the error. Two heads might be better than one but not if they both ended up with a headache!

'She's all ready so go on up. It's the room at the back—the one overlooking the garden.'

Helen stood up when Lewis came back into the kitchen. 'I'll go straight up. I've tried adding everything up again but I'm still getting the wrong answer.'

'I'll check it over while you're reading Kristy a story,' he assured her as he plugged in the kettle. 'I'll put a pot of coffee on first, though, shall I?'

'Please. I'm dying for a drink,' she admitted.

'Me, too. There's nothing like paperwork to give you a thirst...' He stopped and frowned. 'Have you had anything to eat yet tonight?'

'No. I was going to go out and buy myself a sandwich but I didn't bother in the end. I was more concerned about getting this paperwork finished.'

'You can't work on an empty stomach! I'll make you some supper. How about an omelette—would that do?'

'Oh, no, really, you mustn't go to any trouble...'

'It's no trouble at all.' He treated her to another of those engaging smiles. 'I make a really mean omelette, even if I say so myself. You'll be missing a treat if you refuse.'

'In that case, that would be great. Thank you,' she murmured, hurrying out of the door. She paused in the hall while she tried to calm herself down but her heart was racing out of control again and she couldn't understand how a smile could have this much of an effect on her. People smiled at her every day of the week but her heart didn't normally start pounding. However, the minute Lewis smiled at her, it felt as though her entire coronary system had gone into overdrive! It was all very puzzling so she tried not to dwell on it as she made her way upstairs.

Kristy greeted her with delight when she went into her bedroom. 'Will you read me the story about the horse?'

'Of course I will.' Helen went to the bookcase. 'Which one is it?'

'There…on the top shelf.' Kristy pointed to the book she wanted and Helen took it off the shelf.

'Do you want me to start from the beginning?' she asked as she sat down on the bed.

'Yes, please.'

Kristy snuggled up against her and Helen put her arm around her as she started to read. 'Once upon a time there was a beautiful grey mare called Snowflake…'

She read to the end of the first chapter then smiled at the little girl as she closed the book. 'I think that's enough for tonight. It's getting late and you need to go to sleep.'

'All right.' Kristy didn't argue as she lay down. 'Will you read me some more tomorrow night, Helen?'

'I won't be here tomorrow night,' she explained gently, tucking the quilt around her. 'But I'm sure your daddy will read it to you.'

She kissed Kristy on the cheek then switched off the lamp and went downstairs. There was the most delicious smell issuing from the kitchen and she sniffed appreciatively as she went into the room. 'Something smells good.'

'My speciality—cheese and ham omelette.' Lewis lifted a fluffy golden omelette out of the pan and placed it on a plate. He carried it over to the table, bowing as he pulled out a chair for her. '*Voilà!* Supper is served, *madame.*'

'Thank you, Chef.' Helen laughed as she sat down. Picking up the knife and fork he'd laid out for her, she cut off a piece of the omelette and popped it into her mouth. 'Oh, this is delicious! How on earth did you get it so light? Whenever I make an omelette, it's really stodgy.'

'Ah, that's a trade secret.' He winked at her as he sat down. 'And I promised on my honour that I would never divulge it to anyone.'

'Far be if from me to make you break your promise,' she said lightly, determinedly battening down her heart when it immediately responded to the gentle teasing. She concentrated instead on the food, sighing with pleasure when she put down her knife and fork after she'd finished. 'Well, trade secret or not, that has to be the best omelette I've ever eaten.'

'And so it should be. The guy who told me how to make the perfect omelette was a chef at the Savoy so he knew what he was talking about.'

'Oh, I see. I *am* impressed. But how come he told you the secret?' she asked curiously as he cleared away her plate.

'Because I operated on him when he had cancer of the colon.' He picked up the coffee-pot and brought it over to the table. 'Fortunately, the operation was a complete success so he thanked me the best way he knew—by explaining how to make the perfect omelette.'

'What a lovely gesture!' she exclaimed, then sighed. 'It must have been very difficult for you to have to give up such a successful career.'

'I expected it to be harder than it actually was.' He shrugged when she looked at him in surprise. 'I miss the actual surgery part because you get a real buzz after you've operated and saved someone's life. However, I don't miss the rest. There was an awful lot of time wasted on hospital politics and it used to annoy me.'

'It's the same in general practice—so much time is wasted behind the scenes. Every year the paperwork seems to increase and that puts extra pressure on everyone.'

'Which is why it would be a good idea to hire a practice manager to take care of all those irritating jobs that have to be done.' He poured them both a cup of coffee and passed one to her.

'I have to admit it's tempting…'

'But?'

She shrugged. 'But I need to square it with my conscience first.'

'Obviously, that's something only you can decide.'

He picked up the sheet of figures, making it clear that he

wasn't going to try and persuade her. Perversely, Helen found herself wishing that he had. She needed someone to reassure her that she would be doing the right thing...

She brushed aside that thought, annoyed with herself for vacillating. She was a grown woman and she didn't need anyone to make up her mind for her. They set to work again but by ten o'clock they were no closer to finding the problem. Helen ran a weary hand over her face. 'I just don't know where we're going wrong, do you?'

'No. We must have gone over these figures a hundred times by now—' He suddenly broke off and let out a whoop of joy. 'That's it! Right there.'

'Where?' She leant forward and stared at where he was pointing. but she still couldn't see what he meant.

'See, that column on the right is exactly the same as the one on the left but it should be—'

'Four thousand pounds *lower*!' she finished for him. She gave a little whoop of glee. 'We did it. We actually did it!'

'Yep. What a pair of idiots we are not to have spotted it sooner.'

He grinned at her and Helen felt her heart give an almighty lurch when she saw the warmth in his eyes. She knew that she should say something to defuse the moment, but for the life of her she couldn't think what. She could only sit there as though transfixed and maybe she was, too—transfixed by the need to have him look at her like that for ever.

'Helen.'

His voice grated so that her name sounded strange when it emerged from his lips, and she shivered. When he reached across the table and covered her hand with his, she could feel ripples of sensation running up her arm. His hand was so warm and strong—a surgeon's hand with those long, sensitive fingers—and the ripples started to spread as she found herself wondering how it would feel to have his hands on other parts of her body.

The thought stunned her. She'd never wondered before how it would feel to allow a man other than Ian to make love to her, yet that was what she was doing. She was imagining how good it would feel to have Lewis's hands stroking her skin, caressing her breasts, arousing her to a passion she'd never experienced before, and it was just too much.

She leapt to her feet, but he was too quick for her. He was round the table in a trice, gathering into his arms as he forced her to stop. 'Don't! Please, don't run away, Helen. We need to talk…'

'No!' She pushed him away. 'I'm sorry, Lewis, but I don't want to listen to anything you have to say.'

'Then maybe this will convince you.'

Before she realised what he intended, she found herself back in his arms. She just had time to draw a single breath before his mouth found hers and the instant his lips touched hers, she was lost. Helen felt the blood rush to her head. Other kisses she'd shared in the past had been mere tokens compared to this. This kiss touched both her heart *and* her soul, touched her on so many levels that she was powerless to resist.

Lifting her face, she kissed him back with a lifetime's worth of repressed passion. Maybe she had been married but it felt as though she was still the innocent young woman she'd been twelve years ago. It had taken Lewis's kiss to show her what she'd been missing. His kiss had opened the door to a wonder-ful new world, a world where dreams could come true…

CHAPTER NINE

'*DADDY!*'

Lewis flinched when he heard an anguished cry from upstairs. Helen's response had been everything he could have dreamt it would be. She hadn't held back or tried to pretend that she hadn't wanted him to kiss her, but the sound had jolted him back to reality with sickening speed. His daughter was calling for him and he had to go to her!

He let Helen go, feeling his heart ache when he saw the expression on her face. Her eyes were heavy with passion, her mouth was ripe and swollen from his kisses, and he wanted nothing more than to sweep her back into his arms—only he had a child to consider. His precious daughter. The person whom he had sworn to put before all others.

'Kristy's shouting for me,' he explained tersely, turning away. He strode to the door, steeling himself before he glanced back. 'I'm sorry, Helen, but it might be best if you went home.'

'Home?'

The confusion in her voice was almost his undoing, but he knew that he wouldn't be able to live with himself if he let Kristy down. His daughter needed him and he intended to be there for her no matter how difficult it might be for him personally.

'I think it would be best, don't you?' He drummed up a laugh, hoping Helen couldn't tell how much it was hurting him to send her away. 'I don't know what came over me just now. I hadn't

107

planned on making a pass at you, so I can only apologise. It must have been all that effort we put into working out those figures— it turned my head!'

'Don't worry about it.' She turned away, keeping her face averted as she gathered together the papers they'd been using. 'You go and see to Kristy. I'll let myself out. I hope she'll be all right.'

'I'm sure she'll be fine.'

Lewis hesitated but there was nothing more he could say, was there? He left the kitchen and hurried upstairs. Kristy was sitting up in bed with tears streaming down her face so he went straight over and gathered her into his arms. 'It's all right, darling. Daddy's here now. Did you have a bad dream?'

'There was a big truck…'

She buried her face in his chest as the terrors of the nightmare came flooding back, and he sighed. As he'd feared, the episode with the lorry that morning had affected her badly. He gently rocked her to and fro as he tried to soothe her. He heard the back door close and realised that Helen must have left. Even though he knew it was foolish, he couldn't help wishing that he hadn't told her to go. He couldn't bear to imagine what she must think of him now, but there was nothing he could do. He had to put Kristy first after all the heartache she'd been through. Even though she seemed to like Helen, he couldn't risk introducing someone else into her life while she was still so vulnerable. Her world had been turned upside down by the death of her mother and she needed stability more than anything else, not more disruptions.

And, of course, it wasn't just Kristy's life that would be disrupted. What about Helen herself? She, too, was vulnerable, although in a different way. She may have responded to his kiss, but it was obvious that she hadn't got over her husband's death yet. The thought that she might leap into a situation she could come to regret was more than he could bear. He didn't want to be responsible for causing her any pain so maybe it had been better that he'd called a halt when he had?

He tried to convince himself that he'd done the right thing but he couldn't help feeling that he'd let Helen down. He tried to put it out of his mind while he settled Kristy down by reading her another chapter of the book and fetching her a glass of milk. He sat on the side of the bed while she drank it, smiling at her when she handed him the empty glass.

'How do you feel now, sweetheart? Do you think you can try to go to sleep again?'

'I need to go to the toilet first, Daddy,' she told him solemnly.

'Of course you do,' he agreed, knowing it was just a delaying tactic. She was still a bit scared after the nightmare so he played along. 'Off you go, then. I'll wait here so I can tuck you up when you come back.'

'Promise?' she asked, climbing out of bed.

'Cross my heart,' he told her, making the shape of a cross on his chest with his finger.

She giggled as she ran out of the room and he breathed a sigh of relief because the crisis seemed to be over. He smoothed the sheets and plumped up her pillow then tucked her in when she came back from the bathroom. Bending down, he dropped a gentle kiss on her forehead.

'I'll leave the bedroom door open so just shout for me if you need anything.'

'I will.' She snuggled under the quilt. 'Is Helen still here?'

'No, she's gone home now,' he explained, switching off the bedside lamp.

'Oh!'

She didn't say anything else as she closed her eyes so he couldn't tell if she was glad or sorry that Helen had left. Not that it mattered, he told himself sternly as he went to the door. Helen wasn't part of this equation. It was just him and Kristy, and that was how he intended it to continue. However, as he made his way downstairs, he couldn't help wishing that he'd met Helen at a different time in his life. *Then* he might not have needed to send her away.

Helen was late for surgery the following day. She'd spent a sleepless night thinking about what had happened between her and Lewis so it had been almost six when exhaustion had caught up with her and she'd slept right through her alarm call. When she hurried into the office shortly before nine a.m., Janet greeted her with concern.

'I was just about to phone you to see if you were ill.'

'I overslept and didn't hear the alarm going off.'

She picked up the stack of files that were waiting for her, not wanting to be drawn into a discussion. What would Janet think if she told her why she'd not heard the alarm ringing? she wondered as she went to the door. Most probably Janet would be shocked and she would be right to feel that way, too. Kissing Lewis had been a stupid thing to do. Not only could it have an effect on her professional life but it had had a disastrous effect on her personally. She still couldn't believe that she'd compared Lewis to Ian and found her late husband lacking in any way. She had loved Ian, and it had been disloyal of her to criticise him because he hadn't possessed the experience with women that Lewis had.

'Oh, before you go, Helen, there was a message from the hospital for you. The consultant wanted you to know that Lucy Maguire has regained consciousness.'

'That's wonderful!' Helen tried to shrug off the feeling of despondency that had descended on her. 'I'll pop in to see her this afternoon. It's my half-day off today so I'll go straight into town after I finish surgery.'

'You're going to take the afternoon off?' Janet exclaimed in amazement. 'What made you suddenly decide that this place can function without you?'

'Nobody's indispensable,' she said lightly, not wanting to admit that it had been Lewis's comments that had prompted the decision. She didn't want to think about him any more than she had to after last night.

'Well, I'm very glad to hear it.' Janet smiled at her. 'Maybe I shouldn't say this, but I've been really worried about you since the twins went away. You've been working far too hard and it's about time you took some time off.'

'You could be right.'

Helen didn't say anything else as she left the office. However, it was a surprise to discover that even Janet believed that she'd been doing too much. Maybe she would try to reduce the amount of hours she spent in the surgery, she decided as she went into her room. And consider hiring a practice manager. She certainly didn't want to go through a repeat of yesterday's fiasco with those budget figures.

The thought immediately reminded her of what had gone on between her and Lewis, and she frowned. Quite apart from the fact that she felt so bad about comparing Ian to Lewis, there was no denying that she also felt hurt by the casual way Lewis had dismissed that kiss. Maybe it hadn't been special for him but it had been a revelation to her. He had awoken her desire and if he hadn't called a halt, then she certainly wouldn't have done.

Her face flamed as she realised that she would have slept with him if he'd asked her to, but there was no point lying to herself. She'd wanted him that much and knowing how easily he had aroused her meant that she would have to be extra-careful in the future. There was no way on earth that she wanted to make a fool of herself again.

It was a sobering thought and she found it hard to shrug it off as she started on her morning list. Diane Hartley had come in to discuss her test results so Helen went through them with her.

'As I told you briefly over the phone, Diane, the blood tests showed a definite drop in your levels of oestrogen. It confirms my initial diagnosis that you are going through an early meno-pause. That's why you've been experiencing all those distress-ing symptoms recently.'

'So what happens now, Dr Daniels? I mean, there is something you can do to help me, isn't there? Martin will be devastated if I have to tell him that we can never have a family. He's just longing to be a dad.'

'I understand and that's why I don't intend to waste any time. I'm going to refer you to a specialist and let him deal with the problem. I think I mentioned there was a clinic near Blackpool when you first came to see me.'

'That's right,' Diane agreed eagerly. 'Do you think they'll be able to do something?'

'There have been huge advances made over the past few years in fertility treatment. Obviously, I can't promise you a result, just as I can't promise any woman that she will get pregnant. However, this clinic has an excellent reputation for helping women in your position.' Helen smiled at her. 'They are the experts, Diane, and I honestly believe that they will do all they can for you.'

'Then I'm going to give it my best shot,' Diane said firmly. 'I don't care how uncomfortable the treatment is. If there's a way for me to have a baby, I'm going to do my utmost to make it happen.'

'Then I wish you the very best of luck. I know how upsetting this has been for you but at least you know what you're up against now, and that has to be a good thing.'

She saw Diane out, inwardly praying that the treatment would work. No woman should have to suffer the heartache of never having a child if it was what she wanted, she thought as she went back to her desk.

She sighed. It was a fine idea in principle but very difficult to put into practice, as she knew from her own experiences. Just for a moment she found herself imagining how different her life might have been if she hadn't married Ian before she blanked out the thought. She had enough to feel guilty about without going down that route!

The morning wore on. Her lack of sleep meant that Helen had

to concentrate far harder than she normally would have done. She'd always been very conscientious and it troubled her to think that she might miss something because she was so tired. When Tanya Rimmer arrived with her baby son, Dominic, she made sure she gave the young mother her full attention, even though Dominic was screaming so loudly that it was difficult to concentrate.

'Sounds as though this little fellow isn't very happy today,' she said when Tanya came in.

'He's been screaming non-stop since yesterday evening.' Tanya sounded tearful as well as she carried the three-month-old baby into the room. 'My mum said he just had colic and not to fuss, but I wanted to make sure there was nothing really wrong with him.'

'Of course you did. Why don't you lay him on the couch so I can examine him.'

Helen helped her settle the squalling infant on the examination couch. She nodded when she saw how the baby drew up his legs towards his stomach. 'That's a classic sign of colic. Each time his intestines go into spasm it causes him pain and he draws up his legs.'

'So my mum was right after all,' Tanya said tiredly.

'I'll check him over just to make sure.' Helen undid the baby's sleepsuit and gently felt his tummy, murmuring soothingly when he cried even harder. 'There, there, sweetheart, I know it hurts but we'll soon have you feeling better.'

'He cried so hard during the night that he made himself sick,' Tanya explained.

'Really?' Helen frowned. In her experience, vomiting wasn't normally a symptom of colic. 'Have you noticed anything else?'

'Not really... Oh, except there was a bit of blood in his nappy this morning when I changed him.'

'I see.' Helen tucked a blanket around the little boy and smiled at the mother. 'Would you mind waiting here for a moment, Tanya? I want to have a word with Dr Cole about Dominic.'

'Why? What's wrong with him?' the girl demanded anxiously.

'I'd just like a second opinion. It might very well be a simple case of colic but it might be something more than that so it's best to check.'

Leaving Tanya with the baby, Helen hurried along the corridor and knocked on Lewis's door. He had a patient with him and he looked surprised when she popped her head round the door. Helen did her best to behave with her usual composure, although she had to admit that the sight of him had awoken a lot of feelings she could have done without.

'I'm sorry to bother you, Lewis, but I would welcome your opinion on a patient,' she explained formally. 'Perhaps you'd be kind enough to pop along to my room after you've finished?'

'Of course,' he replied equally politely.

'Thank you.'

Helen quickly withdrew, feeling her heart racing as she went back to her room. There was no denying the effect Lewis had on her. Despite her resolve to forget about what had happened last night, it wasn't going to be easy not to think about it. All she could do was hope that she would be able to put it down to experience in time.

Fortunately, there wasn't time to worry about it. Tanya was upset and the baby was screaming harder than ever when she went back to her room. When Lewis arrived a few minutes later, Helen could hardly make herself heard above the din.

'Three-month-old boy exhibiting all the classic signs of severe colic,' she explained when he came over to her.

'But you don't think that's what it is?'

'No.' She shrugged. 'The mother mentioned that he'd been sick and that she'd found blood in his nappy when she'd changed him.'

'Intussusception?' Lewis didn't need her to prompt him towards a diagnosis. His expression darkened as he went to the couch to examine the baby. Peeling off the child's nappy, he pointed to the blood-stained mucus that had collected in it. 'I don't think there's any doubt what it is from that.'

'What do you mean? What's wrong with Dominic?' Tanya demanded, looking scared out her wits. However, before Helen could attempt to calm her, Lewis stepped in. He smiled reassuringly at the young mother.

'We think that Dominic has an obstruction of the bowel called an intussusception. The best way to explain it is to imagine what happens when you try to remove a tightly fitting glove and one of the fingers turns partly inside out. That's what's happened with your son—part of his small intestine has got stuck inside his large one and it needs to be straightened out as quickly as possible.'

'You mean that Dominic will have to have an operation!' Tanya exclaimed, turning white.

'It's possible, although quite often it can be resolved by hydrostatic reduction.' He pulled up a chair and made her sit down. 'Basically, all it means is that Dominic will be given a barium enema and the intestine might right itself because of the pressure of the fluid that's being passed through it.'

'But if it doesn't right itself, he'll need an operation,' Tanya insisted.

'Yes. If nothing is done, the intestine will become permanently blocked and that could have very serious consequences for Dominic. However, I've seen an awful lot of intussusceptions in my time and very often the problem can be resolved without surgery.'

'Does that mean you can do it here?' Tanya asked hopefully.

Lewis shook his head. 'I'm afraid not. Dominic will need to be X-rayed so you'll have to take him to hospital.'

He glanced round and Helen stiffened when she found herself the subject of his gaze. 'Have you any idea who's in charge of gastroenterology at the local hospital?'

'I'm afraid not,' she replied carefully. 'Would you like me to find out for you?'

'Please. I'll give the consultant a call and let him know that we're sending a patient along, to help speed up the process. The sooner this little chap is seen to the better.'

He gave her a quick smile and Helen turned away, not wanting him to know how much the smile had affected her. She quickly left the room, even though she could have found out the information he needed by using the phone on her desk. However, it seemed prudent to put a little distance between them while she got her emotions in check.

A quick call to the hospital's administration department soon achieved the desired results. She made a note of the consultant's name and extension number then went back to her room. Tanya looked a lot calmer when she went in and even managed a smile when she saw Helen, so obviously Lewis had succeeded in reassuring her.

'The consultant's name is John Dancer,' she said, handing him the piece of paper on which she'd jotted down the details.

'John!' He laughed out loud. 'I've known John for years, although I had no idea he was working in this neck of the woods. I'll give him a call and get everything organised.' He turned to Tanya with a smile. 'Dr Dancer is one of the best people in his field so Dominic couldn't be in better hands.'

Tanya looked relieved as he went away to make the call. 'It sounds as though it will be all right, doesn't it, Dr Daniels?'

'I'm sure everything will be fine,' Helen said firmly, because it was ridiculous to feel jealous because Lewis had smiled at the other woman. She helped Tanya to dress Dominic again and they had just finished when Lewis reappeared.

'John is getting everything ready. There'll be an ambulance here in a few minutes to take you to hospital, Tanya, so do you want to phone your husband and let him know what's happening?'

'Andrew's out on a job this morning. He's a site engineer and there's no reception where he's working at the moment so I can't get hold of him on his mobile. Maybe I could phone my mum instead? I'd feel better if I had someone with me,' Tanya added forlornly.

'Of course you would. Come along, then—you can phone her from my room. That way Dr Daniels will be able to see the rest of her patients and I'll be able to keep an eye on this little fellow.' Lewis ushered Tanya to the door then paused. 'Well spotted, Helen. An awful lot of doctors wouldn't have realised what was wrong with this little chap.'

'All part of the service,' she replied lightly, although she couldn't deny that her heart had lifted on hearing the words of praise. As she sat down at her desk, she tried to remember the last time anyone had told her that she'd done a good job. Her patients were always very grateful, of course, but she couldn't recall Ian ever praising her... She shut off that thought. There was no way that she was going to start making any more odious comparisons.

Helen drove straight into town after surgery finished. She parked her car then headed for the coffee-shop. It was market day and the place was full so she ended up sitting on one of the high metal stools at the counter, but she didn't mind. It had been ages since she'd been out for lunch and it was good to watch the world going by.

She paid her bill then decided to browse around the shops before she went to visit Lucy Maguire. She walked along one side of the main street then backtracked along the other, pausing when she came to a small boutique which had opened just before Christmas. She had glanced into the window when she'd been shopping for presents for the twins but she'd been too pressed for time to go in. However, she had time to spare that day so she opened the door.

Thirty minutes later, she left the shop with a glossy carrier-bag in her hand. The clothes had been so gorgeous that she hadn't been able to resist buying herself something to wear. She sneaked a peek at the cobweb-fine pale gold sweater and sighed with pleasure. She'd bought a skirt to go with it—a drift of cloud-soft chiffon in shades of gold and rust. Admittedly the outfit had cost a small fortune but it had looked wonderful on her.

Now all she needed was the right place to wear it and someone who would appreciate it—like Lewis, for instance. What would he think if he saw her in the new outfit?

Her stomach lurched when she realised what she was doing. Closing the carrier-bag, she hurried along the street. She felt both ashamed and guilty that the reason why she'd bought the clothes was so she would look her best for Lewis.

He didn't care how she looked! He'd made that perfectly clear last night when he'd dismissed that kiss they'd shared. She couldn't believe how stupid she'd been to get carried away and made up her mind to return the clothes after she'd been to see Lucy. If the owner of the boutique wouldn't refund her money, she would ask for a credit note and give it to Katie when she came home.

Lucy was still in ICU so Helen went straight up there. Once she'd explained who she was, she was taken through to see her. The nurse who showed her into the unit explained that although Lucy was conscious she still needed careful monitoring so she would be staying in ICU for another couple of days.

Helen thanked her then went to the bed. 'Hello, Lucy. How are you feeling?'

'Sore.' Lucy managed a wobbly smile. 'Every bit of me feels as though it's been trampled on.'

'No wonder!' Helen laughed as she sat down on a straight-backed chair. There were ten beds in the unit and every one was occupied. The muted blips and bleeps of the various monitors provided a background noise. 'Playing chicken with a great big lorry isn't the best start to anyone's day.'

Lucy tried to laugh, then winced as she clutched her throat. 'They put a tube down my throat to help me breathe,' she croaked.

'And I bet it's really sore.' Helen picked up the plastic beaker and helped the girl sip some water. 'I spoke to the social worker yesterday and she told me that your neighbour is looking after your boys. Apparently, she's a registered foster-carer so it was the ideal solution.'

'That's right. Carol…my neighbour…came to see me this morning and she told me the boys were both fine, although they're missing me.' Tears sparkled in Lucy's eyes. 'I just want to get better so I can go home to them.'

'You're making really good progress, Lucy, so it won't be long. You just have to concentrate on getting your strength back.'

Helen glanced round when the same nurse came to tell her that it was time to leave. Visiting was strictly regulated in the unit so she immediately stood up. 'I have to go now but I'll pop in again to see how you are.'

'Thank you. And will you thank Dr Cole for me as well? Carol told me that he stayed under that lorry with me while they got me out. I'm really grateful to him.'

'I'll tell him,' Helen promised, trying to control the warm little glow that had ignited inside her. Lewis had been very brave but it would be silly to think too much about what he'd done.

The intensive care unit was on the fifth floor and there was a queue for the lift when she got there so she decided to use the stairs. She reached the second floor and paused when she saw a sign for the gastroenterology department, wondering if Tanya Rimmer and her baby were still in there. She decided to check so pushed open the door and made her way along the corridor, smiling when she saw Tanya and a fair-haired man coming towards her.

'I was wondering if you were still here.'

'Dr Daniels!' Tanya exclaimed. 'What are you doing here?'

'I've been up to ICU to visit another patient so I thought I'd see how Dominic is doing,' Helen explained, smiling politely at the man.

'He's fine.' Tanya heaved a sigh. 'Dr Dancer has sorted everything out. It was just like Dr Cole said—the enema pushed Dominic's intestine back into its proper place. My mum's with him so I was just on my way to phone Andrew and tell him what's happened. He should be back in his office by now.'

'Oh, that's wonderful news! You must be so relieved, Tanya.'

'I am. I'm also really grateful to you and Dr Cole. Dr Dancer explained how dangerous it would have been if Dominic's condition hadn't been spotted so quickly.'

'So long as he's going to be all right, that's the main thing,' Helen said lightly, turning to the man. 'I'm sorry. I should have introduced myself. I'm Helen Daniels, Tanya's GP.'

'John Dancer, consultant in charge of the gastroenterology unit. I'm delighted to meet you, Helen.' He smiled warmly at her as Tanya excused herself. 'I was most impressed by your rapid diagnosis. A lot of GPs might not have spotted the problem so quickly.'

'I think Lewis deserves the praise more than me. He was the one who confirmed what was wrong with Dominic. I just had my suspicions.'

'Well, it seems you were both very much on the ball, although I wouldn't have expected anything less from Lewis. He knows his stuff—there's no question about that.'

Helen laughed. 'He said exactly the same about you!'

'Obviously a mutual admiration society.' John smiled at her again and Helen felt a little flustered when she saw the appreciation in his eyes. He obviously found her attractive and she wasn't sure how to respond so it was a relief when he carried on.

'I must say that I was surprised to learn that Lewis has switched careers. What made him make such a decision?'

Helen shrugged, unsure what to tell him. She didn't want to betray Lewis's confidence by telling him about Kristy. 'General practice work just seemed more appropriate at the present time.'

'Because of his daughter?' John nodded. 'I heard about that. It must have a been a shock for him, although he's handled it very well. You can only admire a man who's willing to give up a very successful career for the sake of his child.'

'Yes,' she agreed softly. She took a quick breath, trying to quell the rush of emotions the comment had aroused. Lewis's attitude towards his daughter was something else she admired and it was unsettling to be made aware of that in the present circumstances. She didn't want to think about his good points. She didn't want to think about him at all after last night!

'I'll have to get in touch with him again. It would be good to talk over old times.'

'I'm sure he would be pleased to hear from you.' She made a determined effort to concentrate. 'I imagine most of his friends are still living in London so he would probably appreciate having someone to talk to.'

'Then I'll give him a call. Maybe we can arrange to have dinner together...all three of us, I mean.' He smiled at her. 'It would be good to see you again as well, Helen, if it isn't too presumptuous of me to say so.'

'Oh! Well, yes, of course. That would be lovely. Thank you.' Helen quickly covered her confusion by glancing at her watch. 'I really must start heading back. Evening surgery begins at four and I don't want to be late.'

'Of course not. I can get your number from the phone book so I'll give you a call next week.'

'I'll look forward to it,' she said quickly, and held out her hand. 'It's been nice meeting you, Dr Dancer. I'll tell Lewis that you'll be in touch with him.'

'John,' he corrected gently, taking her hand. 'And even if Lewis can't get away for dinner, I'm hoping you will be able to. It would be lovely to see you again, Helen.'

'You, too,' she murmured politely. She said goodbye then made her way back to the stairs, wondering if she'd been right to accept John's invitation. After all, she barely knew him so there was no way of telling if they would have anything in common...

But that's what dates were for, a small voice reminded her. To get to know people and find out if you liked them.

She stopped dead. Had she really agreed to go on a date? She hadn't considered the invitation in that light but that's what it was, of course. Dr Dancer had asked her out because he wanted to spend time with her. He might have included Lewis in the invitation but she wasn't naïve enough to believe that he'd been more interested in catching up with an old friend than seeing her. He was attracted to her and she wasn't sure how she felt about the idea. She certainly didn't know what Lewis was going to think when he found out…

She cut that thought dead. It wasn't any of Lewis's business what she did!

CHAPTER TEN

Lewis could tell something was in the air as soon as he walked into the surgery one day the following week. Janet, Eve and Amy were huddled together in the office, obviously discussing some juicy bit of gossip. He rapped on the door and grinned when the three women leapt apart.

'What are you lot up to? I've never seen such a guilty-looking bunch in my life.'

'We have nothing to be guilty about, have we, girls?' Amy retorted.

'You must think I was born yesterday,' he replied good-naturedly, riffling through the stack of post that was piled on the desk 'All you needed was a bubbling cauldron and you could have passed for the three witches.'

'Cheek! Who are you calling a witch?'

Amy glared at him, although he could tell that she was only pretending to be annoyed. Janet and Eve chuckled as they hurried out to the reception desk to get ready for the morning rush. Obviously, they didn't intend to tell him what had been going on and his curiosity was piqued.

'I apologise. So what's the big secret, then? Something's obviously happened to get you all of a dither.'

'It's Helen,' Amy confided. 'She's got a *date*!'

'A date? You mean with a *man*?'

'No, with an elephant,' Amy shot back in exasperation. 'Of

123

course she's going out with a man. Why do you think we're so excited? I mean, it's the first time she's shown any interest in the opposite sex since Ian died.'

'And that's a good thing?' he asked hollowly, trying to contain all the emotions that were rushing around inside him.

'Of course it's a good thing! You said yourself that she needs a social life, and I think it's great that she's actually going to go out and have some fun for a change.'

'I'm sure you're right.' He summoned a rather sickly smile but the news had left him feeling completely poleaxed. He couldn't begin to explain how it felt to learn that Helen would be spending time with another man when he desperately wanted her to spend it with him. 'So who's the lucky guy, then—do you know?'

'Yes, I do, actually. It's that consultant from the hospital who looked after Tanya Rimmer's baby.'

'You don't mean John Dancer?' he exclaimed.

'That's right. One of my friends works in the gastroenterology department and she says he's really nice. Apparently, he and his wife got divorced a couple of years ago...not because of anything he did,' Amy added hurriedly. 'Their marriage just broke down and he's been single ever since. He'd be perfect for Helen, wouldn't he?'

'John's a decent bloke,' Lewis agreed, struggling to keep a sense of perspective. It wasn't easy so he decided to cut short the discussion before he said something he would regret. 'Anyway, much as I enjoy gossiping with you, Amy, I'd better make a start. Are the others here yet?'

'Helen's in her room but I don't know where Harry's got to...' The nurse broke off when the door opened. 'Speak of the devil.'

Lewis left her and Harry trading friendly insults and made his escape. Helen's door was open and she looked up when she heard him passing. Lewis knew that she'd been avoiding him since the night he'd kissed her so he was rather surprised when she called him into the room.

'I just wanted to check if you're free on Thursday night,' she explained without any preamble. 'John Dancer has invited us both out to dinner at the Forester's Arms. Would you be able to find a babysitter for Kristy?'

'It's unlikely,' he said shortly, thinking that if John had wanted him to go, he would have asked him personally, instead of getting Helen to relay the invitation. Not that he blamed John because he wouldn't have welcomed another man's company if he wanted to spend time with a woman he was interested in.

The thought was a little too near the knuckle and his mouth thinned. 'I haven't used a sitter since we moved here and I really don't want to run the risk of Kristy getting upset if I leave her with a stranger. Tell John thanks but, no, thanks, would you?'

He swung round to leave then stopped when Helen called him back. He could see the puzzlement on her face as she got up from her chair.

'Are you upset about John asking us out?'

'He asked you out, Helen, not me. I was just an afterthought.'

'Oh, no, really, it wasn't like that,' she protested, but he didn't want to hear any more. What was the point of listening to her explain that John Dancer's motives were of the very highest order when he understood exactly what was going on?

'It doesn't matter, Helen. I'm certainly not going to lose any sleep over it so don't give it another thought. John's a nice chap and if you enjoy his company, that's fine. Now, I really must get ready before my patients arrive.'

He left her office and went to his own. He'd only just sat down when Janet buzzed him to ask if she could send in his first appointment. He agreed and settled down to a morning filled with work, yet no matter how hard he concentrated, part of his mind kept niggling away at the thought of Helen and this date she was going on. He didn't want her to go—that was obvious. But he didn't have the right to stop her. That was obvious, too.

* * *

Thursday arrived and all day long Helen was a bundle of nerves. It had been years since she'd been out on a date and she wasn't sure exactly what would happen that evening. She knew that attitudes had changed in the past twelve years but would John expect more of her than she was willing to give?

It was a relief to leave the surgery at the end of the day, not least because of the atmosphere that had descended on the place. Janet, Amy and Eve were so excited about her date that she felt she had to appear upbeat, too. However, Lewis was taciturn to the point of rudeness. He obviously had reservations and she wasn't sure why when he'd stated that his old friend was a decent person. Only Harry seemed untouched by the drama and she was glad of his cheery good wishes to enjoy her evening. At least one of them was behaving like a normal human being!

She went straight home and showered then changed into the new outfit she'd bought in the boutique. She'd not got round to taking it back and she was glad that she hadn't when she stepped in front of the mirror. The sweater was every bit as gorgeous as she remembered, the delicate fabric softly moulding her breasts. The skirt was a swirl of vibrant colour, enhancing the slimness of her calves and ankles. She'd left her hair loose that night and the rich, Titian waves fell around her shoulders in a silky curtain. As she stared at her reflection, Helen had difficulty recognising herself. Was that really her—that tall, elegant and, dare she say it, beautiful woman staring back at her?

She turned away from the mirror as a fresh bout of nerves suddenly kicked in. If it hadn't already been so late, she would have phoned John and cancelled their arrangements. However, good manners dictated that she must go through with it now. Anyway, there really wasn't any reason to worry, she told herself firmly. They were only going for a meal so it wasn't as though anything untoward could happen!

In the event, she needn't have worried because John turned out to be a wonderful companion. Helen's nervousness soon disappeared and she began to enjoy the experience of being fêted by a good-looking man. The time flew past so that she was shocked when she realised that the dining room was empty. They were the last people in there so it was definitely time to call a halt.

John paid the bill then helped her on with her coat. 'I've really enjoyed tonight, Helen. Thank you so much for coming out with me.'

'I've enjoyed it, too,' she said truthfully. She let him take her arm as they left the pub, enjoying the feeling of being cosseted for once. They'd driven there in their own cars and John escorted her back to where she'd parked.

'Maybe we could do it again if you're not too busy?'

'I'd like that.' She smiled up at him, grateful for the fact that he'd been such an easy companion. Maybe he interpreted the smile the wrong way because he suddenly drew her to him and kissed her.

Helen stood quite still, feeling oddly detached. The kiss wasn't unpleasant but it didn't arouse her either. John smiled as he let her go and she was surprised to see no trace of disappointment in his eyes. She could only conclude that he'd been perfectly satisfied by her lack of response.

'I'll say goodnight, then. I'm away at a conference over the weekend so I'll phone you next week, if that's all right?'

'Fine,' she agreed, suddenly eager to bring the evening to a conclusion. She unlocked her car and quickly got in. 'Thank you again for a lovely evening. It's a shame that Lewis wasn't able to join us.'

'I have to confess that I didn't miss his company,' John said wryly.

He closed the door then moved out of the way while she backed out of the parking space. Helen sketched him a wave and headed for the exit, wondering why she'd felt it necessary to mention Lewis. She'd already explained why Lewis hadn't been able to come so why had she brought his name into the conversation? Because John's kiss had been a pale imitation of the one she and Lewis had shared.

Her heart lurched but there was no point lying to herself. She'd felt nothing when John had kissed her yet she'd felt all kinds of emotions when Lewis had done so. His kiss had shown her how passion really felt and, now that she'd tasted the real thing, she would never be able to settle for less. But what if she only responded to Lewis that way? Was she prepared to spend the rest of her life on her own because he didn't want her?

It was impossible to answer that question and Helen sighed. The evening might have been a success but it was going to cause her a lot of problems in the future.

Lewis couldn't settle. Knowing that Helen had gone out with John Dancer had made him feel very on edge. Even though he was sure that his old friend would look after her, it didn't make him feel any better when she was spending time with another man.

What were they doing now? he wondered as he went downstairs after reading Kristy a bedtime story. It was only seventhirty so they'd probably be having a pre-dinner drink. After that, they'd decide what they wanted to eat. It was a first date so it would be an exercise in getting to know one another. John would ask Helen questions about herself and she would reciprocate. The thought that his friend would know more about her than he did by the end of the evening didn't sit well with him, although there was nothing he could do about it. He could hardly have forbidden Helen to share her innermost secrets with any man apart from him!

The thought made him snort with derision because he could just imagine her reaction if he did that. She was an independent woman who had strong views about her life and he wouldn't want her to be any different. In fact, he couldn't think of a single thing he would want to change about her. She was beautiful, intelligent and sexy. If she had a flaw then it was the fact that she worked too hard, and even that was about to change.

Now that she'd set off on the dating merry-go-round, she would have less time to worry about her job. After all, this date was just the first step and there'd be plenty more such occasions once the male members of the population discovered she was available. She would probably be beating them off with a big stick soon, and that thought certainly didn't soothe him. He didn't want Helen to be surrounded by a horde of admirers. He wanted her all to himself!

The thought set the tone for the rest of the evening. He tried to distract himself by watching television but by the time midnight arrived, he'd had enough. He had just switched off the set when the phone rang so he snatched up the receiver before it woke Kristy and was surprised to discover it was the emergency services control centre.

Lewis listened in mounting dismay as the operator explained that there'd been a train crash two miles outside the town. The Beeches was part of the local major incident team and the operator needed to know how many of their staff would be able to respond. Apparently, they'd tried Helen's home phone number and had been unable to get a reply so had contacted him.

'Three definitely plus a possible fourth,' he told the operator, his mind racing. Harry would be a definite yes and Amy, too. He would go as well, although he would have to make arrangements for Kristy to be looked after. As for Helen, well, he would try to reach her on her mobile. If she was able to respond then all well and good, but if not he'd leave her to whatever she was doing...

He blanked out that thought, not wanting to think any more about what she might be doing with John Dancer. He gave the operator the names of all the personnel who would be on their team then set about contacting them. Harry offered to collect Amy so that solved the problem of how the nurse would get to the accident scene.

Lewis phoned Amy next, sighing when she asked him what he was going to do about Kristy. 'All I can think of is to bring her with me and leave her in the control centre, although I can't say I'm happy about the idea.'

'How about if I ask my mum to come round and babysit for you?' Amy suggested. 'She only lives a few minutes away from you and I know she wouldn't mind.'

'That would be great!' He thanked Amy and hung up then dialled Helen's mobile phone. The answering service cut in after half a dozen rings so he left a message then broke the connection. Where Helen was and what she was doing was her business, and he wasn't going to make the mistake of speculating about it…

Like hell he wasn't!

His expression was grim as he went upstairs to get ready. It didn't take a great deal of effort to work out that Helen must have enjoyed the evening so much that she'd decided to prolong it. It was gone midnight and there were very few places where she could be at this time of the night. One of them was at home in her own bed, but she would have answered when the emergency services had telephoned her if that had been the case. The second option was far more likely in his view: she'd gone back to John's house and was spending the night there. The thought of what might be happening was something he really didn't want to think about, and he groaned. What a mess this was turning into!

Helen was on her way home when she heard about the train crash on the radio. She immediately turned the car round and headed back the way she'd come. The accident had happened not far from where she'd had dinner, at a spot where the railway track ran alongside the motorway, so she didn't waste any time as she drove to the site. She had to pull over onto the verge to allow a convoy of fire engines to pass her and her heart sank. The number of vehicles that had been dispatched to the scene proved it must be a major incident.

She rounded a bend and screeched to a halt at the sight that met her. The train had completely derailed and there were several carriages lying at the bottom of the bank. Fire had broken out and the smoke from it had drifted across the northbound carriageway of the motorway, causing dozens of cars to crash. It was like a scene from a disaster film and she knew that there were going to be many casualties that night.

She drove as close to the accident site as she could get, lowering her window when a policeman flagged her down. 'I'm a doctor,' she explained, taking her ID out of her bag and showing it to him. 'I'm part of the major incident team for this area of Lancashire.'

'We could certainly do with your help, Doc.' The policeman pointed to a nearby field. 'Can you park in there? We need to keep the road clear for the ambulances and other emergency vehicles.'

'Of course.' Helen pulled off the road, the wheels of her car sliding in the mud as she parked at the end of the row of vehicles. Pushing her handbag into the glove-box, she got out and went round to the boot. She kept a spare medical bag in there for emergencies, along with a pair of Wellington boots and some old overalls which would come in very useful that night. She was just fastening back her hair with an elastic band when another car drew up and two doctors from a practice in a neighbouring town got out.

Helen greeted them then they all made their way to the command centre and reported to the officer in charge, who was liaising with the various emergency services. She nodded when she was asked to attend to the walking wounded. She knew from the training she'd received that the key to successfully controlling a major incident was to delegate a task to each member of the team. Everyone needed to know what they should be doing at every given point in the proceedings to avoid chaos ensuing.

The injured had been gathered close to the railway embankment. There was a young WPC with them and she looked relieved when Helen introduced herself. She did a quick assessment, working her way from one casualty to the next to find those who were the most severely injured and in the most danger. There was a mother and a young child near the middle of the group and they both appeared dazed when she knelt down beside them.

'I'm Helen and I'm a doctor. Can you tell me where you're hurt?'

'My hand…'

The mother looked vaguely at her right hand. Helen grimaced when she saw that it had been severed just above the wrist. All that was left was a stump of bone showing through the flesh.

'That needs covering up,' she said briskly, taking a dressing out of her case. Fortunately, someone had had the sense to use a pressure pad to control the bleeding so she carefully wrapped the wrist in a sterile dressing then fashioned a sling and elevated the whole arm. 'The ambulances will be here very shortly and you'll be taken straight to hospital. Is there anything else? What about your daughter?'

'I don't know…' The woman looked at her with shock-blank eyes. 'We were having a drink of tea and the next moment there was this terrible noise.'

'It must have been awful,' Helen said softly, wishing there was more she could do for the poor soul. She turned to the little girl, seeing the same frozen expression of horror on the child's face. 'Do you hurt anywhere, sweetheart? Your arms or your legs…anywhere at all?'

The child shook her head but Helen didn't want to take any chances. She quickly examined her but, from what she could tell, miraculously she hadn't suffered any injuries apart from a small bruise on her temple.

'Did you pass out when the accident happened?' she asked the child, taking out her torch and shining it into her eyes. Another shake of the head was all the answer she got, but as there was no other indication of any head trauma, she had to accept it. However, as she moved to the next person, she made a note to check on the child again just to be on the safe side.

She worked her way through the group, treating the most severely injured and doing her best to reassure those who were in no immediate danger. They were all in shock and all traumatised by what had happened. One man was having severe chest pains and she guessed that he was in the throes of a heart attack. She administered analgesics and a thrombolytic drug to dissolve any blood clots then went back to her car for the oxygen cylinder she always carried with her. He looked a little better by the time she'd finished and she was fairly confident that he would survive until the ambulances arrived, which they did a short time later.

Helen went to meet the paramedics who had been assigned to her. She wanted them to take the mother and child first, along with the heart-attack victim. She helped the crew load them on board then got the next group ready. There were more people being sent to her as the fire crews freed them from the carriages so she started on a second round, prioritising the most severely injured so they could be treated first.

She'd just finished when she happened to glance up and saw Lewis walking towards her. There was the strangest expression on his face, a mixture of relief and some other emotion she couldn't determine but which made her legs tremble as she stood up. She wasn't sure what was going on but there was definitely something happening, as was proved the moment he spoke.

'How long have you been here?' he demanded in a voice taut with emotion.

'I'm not sure. A couple of hours, I imagine. Why?'

'I tried to get hold of you but your phone wasn't switched on.'

'Wasn't it?' She sighed. 'I switched it off while we were having dinner and I must have forgotten to turn it on again after I heard about the accident. I was on my way home when they announced it on the local radio station so I drove straight over here.'

'I see.' He glanced round when there was a shout from the embankment. 'Looks like they've found someone in those carriages. I'd better get back and see what I can do.'

'Is Harry here as well?' Helen demanded hastily, loath to let him leave.

'Yes, and Amy, too. They're up on the motorway, helping with the injured drivers. I've been deployed with the rapid response unit from the local hospital.'

'So you're in the thick of things.'

She shivered as she glanced towards the train. The firemen were using oxyacetylene torches to cut through the metal and get at the people who were trapped inside. It was dangerous work because the carriages were very unstable and she hated to think of Lewis putting himself at risk.

'Just doing what I can to help,' he said lightly, dismissing the danger.

'Be careful, though, won't you?' She bit her lip when she heard the fear in her voice because she knew that he must have heard it, too.

'I will.' He looked at her and his eyes were very grave when they met hers. 'You be careful, too, Helen. I don't want anything happening to you.'

Helen didn't say anything. She simply couldn't think of an appropriate reply and he didn't seem to expect one. He turned and walked away, and she watched him climbing up the embankment until he disappeared into the crowd.

She took a deep breath then returned to what she'd been doing. She knew she couldn't think about what had happened when there were people depending on her for help. However, later, she would let herself remember the way Lewis had looked at her as though she was the most precious thing in his life. Maybe it had meant something and maybe it hadn't, but it definitely needed thinking about.

It was almost four a.m. when the operation began to wind down and all the casualties had been transferred to hospital. There were still a few people left in the carriages but there was nothing anyone could do to help them.

Lewis couldn't remember ever having felt so tired as he made his way back to the command centre to sign off. Every muscle in his body ached from the exertion of squeezing through gaps no human being was meant to fit through. Harry and Amy joined him at the makeshift desk, their usual banter subdued by the sights they'd witnessed that night. There were fifteen dead from the train crash and another six from the motorway pile-up so one way or another it had been a bad night for a lot of people.

'It's been tough,' he observed, filling in the time of his departure.

'Tell me about it.' Harry looked grim as he filled in his own details. 'I don't fancy another night like this in a hurry.'

'Me neither,' Amy agreed. She took the pen from Harry and scrawled her signature on the sheet. 'I'm so tired I can hardly sign my own name!'

'Good job you aren't writing me a cheque then,' Harry joked, making a brave stab at humour.

Lewis grinned tiredly as he followed them along the road. 'You two should form a double act and go on the stage. You'd earn a fortune!'

'I might consider it after tonight. There has to be an easier way to make a living,' Harry retorted, glancing round as Helen came over to join them. 'Hi! It's been quite an eventful night, hasn't it?'

'It has indeed,' she agreed, falling into step with them.

Lewis didn't say anything, even though he agreed wholeheartedly with the sentiment. It had been an eventful night and not just because of the train crash either. He sighed because there was no point pretending why he'd been so relieved to see Helen at the accident site that night. Maybe it was selfish, but the fact that she'd been there and not with John had taken a weight off his mind. He knew he was acting like the proverbial dog in the manger, but the thought of her spending the night with another man was more than he could bear. He didn't want her to spend the night with anyone else. He wanted her to spend it with him!

He coughed as all the air suddenly exploded from his lungs, and she turned to him in concern. 'Are you all right?'

'I'm fine,' he spluttered. He made himself breathe in then out but his chest still felt as tight as a drum after he'd finished. It was no wonder, too. Thoughts like that were extremely hazardous to one's health, but he couldn't seem to control his mind now that it had been allowed a little leeway.

He wanted to spend the night with Helen and fall asleep with her in his arms. He wanted to hold her close and listen to the sound of her breathing, secure in the knowledge that he would relive the experience the next night and every night after that. That was what it all boiled down to. He didn't want to spend just one night with her—he wanted a whole lifetime's worth of nights, and he'd never wanted that with any woman before. What did it mean? Was it possible that he'd fallen in love with her?

'That's it, folks. I'm off home to my bed!'

Harry waved as he climbed into his car, and Lewis realised with a start that they'd arrived at the car park while he'd been daydreaming. He managed to respond when Amy shouted good-bye but his head was pounding from the effort of trying to sort out his feelings. Was he in love with Helen? Or was he misinterpreting the depth of his feelings for her because he was so tired?

'We'll be like zombies in the morning.' Helen stopped beside her car and zapped open the lock. She looked at him in concern when he didn't answer. 'Are you sure you're feeling all right?'

'Not really.' He drummed up a smile, hoping it would put her off the scent because he didn't want to explain why he was behaving so strangely. 'I'm so tired that I could lie down right here on the ground and go to sleep.'

'I know how you feel.' His answer seemed to have reassured her because she didn't question him further as she got into her car. 'I'll see you tomorrow at the surgery…if you make it, of course.'

'I'll do my best.'

He gave her a quick smile then carried on along the row until he came to his own car. Unlocking the door, he got in and started the engine, only to discover that the wheels were firmly stuck in the mud when he tried to drive off. Easing the car into reverse, he tried to back out but only succeeded in digging it even deeper into the mire.

Switching off the engine, he put his head on the steering-wheel in defeat. He was well and truly stuck in the mud, and it couldn't have been a more fitting end to the night!

CHAPTER ELEVEN

THE sound of a car horn made him look up. Lewis sighed when he realised that Helen had pulled up alongside him. Rolling down the window, he smiled ruefully at her. 'I'm stuck in the mud. Do you think you could tow me out?'

'I've not got a tow rope with me. How about you?'

'Nope.' He glanced around, but the field was almost empty. They were among the last vehicles to leave so it didn't look as though there would be help coming from any other quarter. He turned to her again and grimaced. 'I hate to ask but would you mind giving me a lift? I'd stay here for the night, but I don't want Kristy waking up in the morning and discovering I'm missing. Amy's mother is with her, but she might be frightened if I'm not there.'

'Of course I don't mind!' She opened the car door and waited while he retrieved his case from his boot. 'Have you got everything you need?' she asked as he climbed in beside her.

'I think so.' He patted his pockets to check that he had his house keys and nodded. 'All present and correct so it's home now, please, James.'

Helen laughed. 'And don't spare the horses, eh?'

'Something like that.' He smiled back then looked away when he felt his heartbeat quicken. It wasn't easy to behave sensibly but he had to get a grip. The thought that he might have fallen in love with her was a lot to contend with, but he had to stick to his decision to put Kristy's happiness above everything else.

'Thank heavens for that,' Helen exclaimed as they left the field. 'I thought I was going to get stuck as well for a moment.'

She picked up speed as soon as they were safely back on the road. There were still a lot of vehicles parked near the railway track and he watched in awe as a huge crane was backed into position.

'Is that really the time?' Helen exclaimed, glancing at the dashboard clock. 'It doesn't seem worth going home when we'll be back at work in a couple of hours, does it?'

'At least we'll have time for a shower,' he replied evenly. So long as they stuck to trivialities, he should be able to manage, he assured himself, so he summoned a smile. 'I don't know about you but I'm dying to wash some of this filth off me.'

'I know what you mean.' She grimaced as she took her hand off the steering-wheel and inspected it. 'I don't know how I got so dirty when I was wearing gloves. Thank heavens I had these overalls with me, otherwise my clothes would have been ruined. I wouldn't mind, but I was wearing a new outfit tonight, too.'

'It was lucky you had them,' he agreed, although his heart had plummeted. Obviously, Helen had made a special effort for her date that night and it wasn't the most cheering news he'd ever had.

'I always keep a pair of overalls in the car, along with my boots,' she explained, pulling up outside his house and smiling at him. 'The life of a GP is far removed from what you see depicted in all those television dramas. They make it look as though we enjoy a non-stop round of glamorous cocktail parties!'

'I wish.' Lewis made a determined effort to appear up-beat as he opened the door. After all, he was the one who'd encouraged her to go out and enjoy herself so he could hardly complain if she'd taken his advice. 'Thanks again for the lift. I'm sorry to have taken you out of your way.'

'You didn't take me out of my way! It's only a couple of minutes from here to my house. What's happening about Amy's mother, by the way? Will she be staying the night or going home now that you're back?'

'I'm not sure,' he admitted, frowning. If Mrs Morris wanted to return home then he would have to go with her, although he didn't know what he was going to do about Kristy. Helen must have realised his dilemma because she switched off the engine.

'Why don't you find out what she wants to do? I'll wait here in case she needs a lift home.'

'Oh, I couldn't possibly expect you to start ferrying her around at this time of the night.'

'You don't have a choice. Your car's stuck in that field and you can't leave Kristy on her own while you walk Mrs Morris home.'

He sighed. 'No. I can't. Look, why don't you come in while we sort it out? There's no point you sitting out here, is there?'

'Well, if you're sure…'

Helen got out of the car when he nodded. She followed him up the path and waited while he unlocked the front door. The hall light was on so he led the way to the sitting room.

'I'll just see where Mrs Morris is.' He pointed to the tray of drinks on the sideboard. 'Help yourself to a drink while you're waiting.'

'I'd much rather have a cup of tea,' she admitted, and he chuckled.

'So would I.'

'Then I'll put the kettle while you check what Amy's mother wants to do.'

Lewis didn't argue. It didn't seem worth making a fuss and if she wanted to make them both some tea, why not let her? He went upstairs and checked on Kristy first, relieved to see that the little girl was fast asleep. His next stop was the guest room and he didn't need to go in: the sound of snoring was enough to tell him that Amy's mother had settled down for the night.

He went back downstairs to the kitchen. Helen was pouring boiling water into the teapot and she glanced round when he came into the room.

'All quiet?'

'They're both fast asleep so I'll take it that Mrs Morris will be staying the night.'

'No point waking her,' she agreed, carrying the pot over to the table. She went back for the mugs then slumped down on a chair. 'I am absolutely shattered! I ache in places I've never ached before.'

'Me, too,' he admitted, thinking how true a statement it was. He did ache, and not just physically either. He ached emotionally as well, although it seemed prudent not to mention that fact. He nodded his thanks when she handed him a mug of tea.

'Oh, drat! I've forgotten the milk.'

'I'll get it.' He stood up at the exact moment she did so and they ended up bumping into one another. He grabbed hold of her arms when she staggered back. 'Sorry! I didn't mean to knock you over in the rush.'

'That's all right.'

She smiled up at him, and in that second Lewis knew he was lost. Every single thought he'd had about behaving sensibly suddenly fled. All he could think about was the fact that Helen was standing in front of him and that all it would take was the tiniest effort to pull her into his arms...

He wasn't aware of moving but all of a sudden his arms were around her and hers were around him. He could feel the softness of her body, smell the scent of her skin, hear the rapid sound of her breathing, and it tipped him over the edge. He didn't even pause as he bent and kissed her, didn't stop to wonder if it was right or wrong because it no longer mattered. He needed this kiss. He needed Helen. And, by heaven, he was going to have her!

Their mouths collided with more speed than finesse but nothing could spoil the magic of their initial contact. When her mouth immediately opened under his, Lewis felt a surge of pleasure hit him. He didn't need to tease or coax her because her passion was every bit as potent as his own. Helen wanted this kiss as much as he did, and it was the only affirmation he needed.

He pulled her to him, letting her feel the strength of his desire, and heard her gasp. His body was pulsing with need, his blood heating to a degree which shouldn't have been possible, yet he could *feel* it happening. When he withdrew his mouth from hers so he could shower kisses across her cheek and along her jaw, she murmured in encouragement, tiny sounds that made his vision blur and his heart pound at double its normal speed.

'I can feel your heart racing,' she murmured, placing her palms flat against his breastbone.

'I know. It's racing for you.' He placed his hand on her breast, felt her nipple harden, and groaned.

'Mine is racing, too,' she whispered, turning her head so that she could nibble at his neck.

Lewis shuddered as a wave of sensation washed through him. It was more than lust, far more than desire, much more than any-thing he'd experienced before, and it filled him with awe. He would never have believed it was possible to feel such depth of emotion but, then, he'd never been on the brink of making love to a woman he loved before.

The thought brought tears to his eyes as he drew her to him and held her against his heart. 'I want to make love to you prop-erly, Helen.'

'It's what I want, too,' she said simply.

'Are you sure?' He set her from him, needing to be sure that she understood exactly what he was suggesting, and she nodded gravely.

'Quite sure.'

She pulled his head down towards her again and kissed him, softly, deeply and with a wealth of passion, and any doubts he had immediately disappeared. She knew exactly what she was doing because it was what she wanted, too.

Taking her by the hand, he led her upstairs to his bedroom. He closed the door, feeling his heart swell with tenderness when he saw her standing there in the centre of the room. Even though he was sure that she didn't have any doubts about what they were doing, he could tell she was nervous and understood why. It was a big step for them to take and he was nervous, too.

Reaching out, he pulled her into his arms and kissed her gently on the mouth, feeling how she immediately relaxed against him. When his hands went to the zip down the front of her overalls, she smiled up at him.

'Do you need a hand to get me out of these? They can be rather tricky.'

'And spoil my fun?' He grinned at her. 'I don't think so!'

Helen chuckled as he ran the zipper down a scant few millimetres. 'Far be it from me to be a spoilsport.'

Lewis dropped an approving kiss on her nose then slid the zip right down to the bottom of its track. Actually getting her out of the overalls was a bit more difficult but the whole exercise was eased by several dozen kisses. Each time he managed to free her from a bit more of the cloth, he stole a kiss so it was a pleasure rather than a chore and definitely worth the effort, he decided when she stepped out of bulky garment. The sight of her dressed in the glorious sweater and skirt was enough to strike him dumb.

Helen giggled. 'It was worth the time it took just to see your reaction. I take it that you like my outfit?' She gave a little twirl and he groaned as he watched the skirt flirting around her gorgeous legs.

'I love it!' he growled, pulling her back into his arms, only this time she resisted.

'Naughty, naughty,' she said reprovingly, wagging her finger at him. 'You've had your fun—now it's my turn.'

Lewis wasn't sure what she meant at first, but he soon found out. He gasped when he felt her hands slide under his sweater as she eased it off him. Her fingers were cool and supple as they stroked his skin and she took her time, letting her hands slide up his body as she worked the sweater up an inch or so at a time. He was trembling by the time it reached shoulder level and was in serious danger of exploding. Grasping the neck of the sweater, he dragged it over his head and tossed it on the floor.

'My turn now,' he grated, not giving her a chance to argue as his hands homed in on her sweater. The fabric was cobweb fine and he groaned when he felt the threads snagging on his fingers. 'Maybe I'd better let you do it instead. I don't want to ruin it.'

'If you insist.'

She stepped back and gently drew the sweater over her head. She placed it on the end of the bed then took the elastic band out of her hair. Lewis gulped. He couldn't recall ever seeing anything as lovely in his entire life. Her body was slender but rounded, her full breasts straining at the lacy cups of her white bra. In the soft glow from the bedside lamp her skin had a pearly sheen that entranced him and provided the most wonderful contrast to the richness of her hair.

Reaching out, he traced his fingers over her collar-bone, feeling the delicacy of the bones beneath the lustrous skin. She was beautiful both inside and out, and he wanted her more than he'd wanted anything in his entire life.

'You're so beautiful,' he whispered, his voice trembling.

'So are you,' she said just as quietly. She laid her hands on his chest, splaying her fingers so that they brushed delicately over his nipples, and he groaned. When she did it a second time, he couldn't contain himself any longer.

He swept her into his arms and kissed her, showing her through his actions how he felt because words weren't enough any more. Words couldn't describe this desperation he felt to make her his. It was as though he had waited his whole life for this moment and now that it had arrived he could scarcely believe what he was feeling. It didn't seem possible that he could want her this much and survive!

Helen twined her arms around his neck and held him just as tightly as he was holding her. Her body was warm and pliant in his arms, her heart racing in time with his. When he lifted her and laid her on his bed, she gave a little murmur, as though she, too, wasn't sure if she could weather this storm of passion they were creating together.

Lewis stripped off the rest of her clothes, although his hands were gentle despite his urgency to see her naked. She was far too precious to him to risk hurting her by being rough so he was careful when he removed her skirt and laid it aside, even more careful as he freed her breasts from the lacy bra. Only then did he allow himself to actually touch her and he couldn't control the gasp that escaped his lips when he felt the softness of her breasts nestling into his palms. She was exquisite, more beautiful and more desirable than any woman he had ever known—but, then, he'd never been in love before.

'Make love to me.'

She whispered the command in his ear and he froze. There was no denying that her passion was equal to his own and for a moment he was terrified by it. What if she was disappointed by his love-making? It had been a long time since he'd slept with a woman and he might not be able to satisfy her, even though he would do everything in his power to make the experience as memorable for her as it would be for him. But would his skills as a lover be enough to give her pleasure?

'Lewis?' She pushed against his chest, making a little space between them, and he knew that he couldn't lie when he saw the worry in her eyes.

'I don't want you to be disappointed,' he admitted, wondering if it would diminish him in her eyes to confess his fears.

'Of course I won't be disappointed! How could I be?' She kissed him on the mouth and the certainty in her eyes was all the reassurance he needed. Helen believed in him and he wouldn't let her down!

They made love with a passion that touched his heart and his soul. Lewis knew that he'd never experienced anything like it before and that he wouldn't experience it again unless it was with her. Despite her obvious desire for him, she was a little hesitant at first, and he was surprised until he realised that it was her lack of experience that was making her hold back. And once he understood that, he was able to overcome it.

Teaching her how to respond to him was the sweetest of pleasures, yet he also learned from her, too. She was so generous, so giving, that he realised he'd never really understood what making love meant. What he'd experienced in the past had been sex. This was different. This took the whole concept to a new level. When they finally fell asleep in each other's arms, his last thought was that he'd just been shown a glimpse of heaven. And from this point on, heaven with Helen was all he would ever want.

Morning sunlight spilled through the window and Helen woke up. She couldn't have had more than a couple of hours' sleep but she felt marvellous. Rolling onto her side, she looked at Lewis lying beside her and sighed.

It was all because of him, of course. Making love with Lewis had been the most wonderful experience of her life and she didn't regret what had happened. However, she couldn't help feeling a little sad because it had shown her what she'd been missing before. She'd always believed that her marriage to Ian had been a happy one, and it had been in many ways. Nevertheless, she'd never felt as fulfilled as she did at that moment and she knew why.

She had loved Ian but she hadn't been in love with him. The problem was that she'd been very young and inexperienced when she'd met Ian and, she realised now, confused about the true nature of her feelings. The fact that her parents had died a few months before she'd arrived at The Beeches had been another factor, too. Ian had offered her the comfort and security she'd needed so desperately at the time. He had been a good man and she'd respected him, but she had never been in love with him. It felt good to face the truth at last, especially when it could have a bearing on her relationship with Lewis.

Lewis's eyes suddenly opened and she jumped. A little colour touched her cheeks when she realised that he'd caught her staring at him. It was all very well for her to speculate about the future but there was no guarantee that he was interested in having a relationship with her. Last night might have been a one-off for all she knew, and the thought made her stomach churn with apprehension.

'Good morning, and how are you today?' His voice was thickened with sleep but she heard the passion it held and some of her fear dissipated. And when he pulled her over onto his side of the bed and kissed her, the rest disappeared as well. She laughed, realising how foolish she had been to worry.

'Very well, thank you. How about you?'

'Good in parts but not so good in others,' he replied, completely deadpan.

'What do you mean?' she said anxiously, propping herself up on her elbow. 'Did you hurt yourself last night at the train crash?'

'No, I survived that intact. It's other bits of me that are aching this morning.' He pulled her down to him and she gasped when she felt the hardness of his erection pressing against her. 'Is there anything you could recommend for this complaint, Dr Daniels?' he asked, smiling into her eyes.

'Cold showers are supposed to be very effective,' she told him in her most professional tone.

'Are they?' He pulled a face. 'I'm not a lover of cold water so maybe there's an alternative…?'

Helen chuckled as he set about solving the problem the best way he knew—one she definitely approved of! Their love-making was both passionate and tender, showing her a whole new range of emotions as well as ways to express them. She could have stayed in his arms for ever but there was a point where life had to intrude.

Lewis groaned when they heard footsteps on the stairs. 'It sounds as though Kristy is awake. I'd better go and see what she's up to.'

He tossed back the quilt and stood up. Taking a pair of pyjama trousers out of a drawer, he pulled them on then handed her his robe. Helen hurriedly slipped it on and got out of bed.

All of a sudden she felt very self-conscious about being there. She knew how curious children could be and she didn't want to put him in the difficult position of having to explain her presence to Kristy, or to Amy's mother, for that matter. Her heart sank because suddenly there seemed to be all sorts of factors to take into account.

'You can use the *en suite*.' He opened a door and showed her the bathroom leading off the bedroom. 'It will give you a bit more privacy than the other one.'

'Thank you,' she responded politely, wondering if he felt as uncomfortable as she did. Obviously, he didn't want anyone to know she was there otherwise he wouldn't have suggested she should use his bathroom, and the thought made her feel more awkward than ever.

'I'll get dressed and slip away while Kristy is having her breakfast,' she offered.

'Would you mind? I know how it must seem, but I'd rather she didn't know you'd stayed here last night.'

'I understand,' she assured him, and it was true. Last night had been a wonderful experience for both of them and she wouldn't denigrate it by thinking it hadn't meant anything to him. However, one night of passion didn't constitute a commitment and she didn't want him to get the wrong idea about her expectations.

'I'd prefer it if nobody knew I stayed either.' She shrugged when he looked at her. 'I don't want people gossiping about us. It could have a detrimental effect on the reputation of the surgery and that's the last thing I want to happen.'

'Of course. I understand completely.'

His tone was flat so she wasn't sure why she felt a ripple of alarm scud through her. She tried to shrug off the feeling as she went into the bathroom and turned on the shower. There was no point looking for problems that might not exist.

It took Helen just ten minutes to shower and dress. Rolling up the overalls, she tucked them under her arm and made her way downstairs. She could hear voices coming from the kitchen but she didn't pause as she quietly let herself out of the house. Lewis had made it clear that he didn't want Kristy to see her and she wasn't going to make life difficult for him. As she got into her car, she told herself that she didn't mind, but in her heart she knew that some of the magic had faded. All she could hope was that they could find a way around the problem.

Lewis desperately wished that he hadn't allowed Helen to slip away. It had made it appear as though their night together had been something shameful. However, until he knew how Kristy would react to the idea of him having a relationship, he had to err on the side of caution.

And Kristy's reaction wasn't the only consideration, was it? Helen had seemed just as reluctant to go public. She claimed that she didn't want people gossiping about them, but was that the only reason? Wasn't it far more likely that she felt *guilty* about betraying her late husband's memory?

The thought was very hard to accept. Lewis knew that he had to make her understand that she'd done nothing wrong. Even though he couldn't make her any promises about the future, he couldn't bear to think that last night had been the beginning and the end for them.

He got Kristy ready as soon as Mrs Morris left and took her to school because he didn't want to give Helen time to brood. Amy was crossing the car park when he arrived at the surgery and she stopped to wait for him.

'You don't look too bad, considering the amount of sleep you had. What's your secret?'

'Clean living,' he replied drolly, following her into the building.

'I don't think! I'd say it was down to practice. You've spent so many nights out on the tiles that now you *thrive* on very little sleep!'

'What can I say?' he responded, elbowing the staffroom door open. 'Obviously, you've sussed me out.'

'Too right I have!' Amy stalked past him. 'I have my spies,

and all I can say is that the number of girlfriends you're reputed to have had would make the average male look like a non-starter! Isn't that right, Helen?'

Lewis's stomach lurched when he realised that Helen was sitting at the table, listening to them. He could see the pain in her eyes before she looked away.

'What Lewis does in his private life is his business,' she said flatly.

Amy looked embarrassed by the reproof but it was nothing to how he felt. The last thing he wanted was Helen thinking that he had a queue of women lined up to sleep with him!

'I'm afraid my reputation has been greatly exaggerated. I wouldn't believe half of what you've heard.'

'I was only joking anyway,' Amy said hurriedly, taking off her coat. She hung it on the rack then scuttled out of the room.

Lewis sighed as he watched her go. 'She didn't mean any harm. It was just a bit of fun.'

'I'm sure it was.' Helen stood up and walked to the door. She barely glanced at him and it hurt unbearably to be treated with such indifference after what they'd shared.

'I'm sorry if I've made life difficult for you,' he said harshly. 'However, I'm not sorry about what happened last night. That is something I certainly don't regret.'

'I think it would be best if we forgot about it, don't you?'

'No, I don't. It happened, Helen, and there is no way you can erase it from your mind because you feel guilty—'

'Why should I feel guilty?' she demanded, glaring at him.

'Because of Ian, of course. I understand how you feel, Helen, but there's no need to blame yourself for being disloyal to his memory.'

'I don't!'

'Then why are you so keen to avoid anyone finding out about us?' he said sceptically.

'Because I don't like the thought of people gossiping about my private life! Anyway, I'm not the only one who wants to keep this quiet. You don't seem exactly eager to shout it from the roof-tops!'

He winced when he felt the sting of that comment. 'No, I'm not, although it isn't because I'm worried what people will say. Kristy is still very vulnerable and I don't know how she will react to the idea of me having a relationship. I won't risk doing anything that might upset her.'

'Then it's a good job that nobody will ever find out what happened, isn't it?'

She went to open the door but he couldn't let her leave like this. He could tell how hurt she was and the last thing he'd wanted to do was to hurt her. Reaching out, he covered her hand with his. 'Last night meant the world to me, Helen.'

'Did it?'

She looked up at him with eyes that were brimming with tears and he groaned as he pulled her into his arms and cradled her against him.

'Yes. You know it did!'

'I don't know anything any more,' she whispered, and his heart ached when he heard the confusion in her voice.

'You know how much I want you,' he said softly, dropping a kiss on her hair. 'I've never wanted anyone this way before, and that's the truth.' He tilted her chin so he could look into her eyes, and heard her sigh.

'And I've never wanted anyone this way either.'

'Then we have to find a way to see each other. It won't be ideal but it will be better than the alternative.' His voice broke. 'I don't think I can bear not to be with you, Helen, even if it's only for a few moments snatched out of each day.'

'And what about Kristy? What if she finds out?'

'She won't—if we're careful.' He smiled into her eyes, wishing with his whole heart that he could offer her more. Helen deserved better than what he was suggesting, but his hands were tied. He couldn't and wouldn't put his own happiness above that of his daughter.

'I don't want to do anything that could hurt her, Lewis. She's been through too much already.' She paused and he could hear the ache in her voice when she continued. 'I'd rather we stopped seeing each other than cause her any distress.'

'Thank you.' He held her close, loving her more than ever at that moment for being so understanding. He longed to tell her how he felt but he knew it wouldn't be fair to do that. He couldn't bind her to him with declarations of love when he couldn't make her any promises about the future.

The thought was so bitter that he couldn't stand it. He dropped a gentle kiss on her mouth then let her go. 'I'd better start as I mean to continue. From now on I shall be a model of good behaviour when we're in the surgery.'

'Not too good, I hope. People are going to be very suspicious if you stop badgering me about the amount of work I do.'

'I don't badger you!' he retorted, then sighed. 'Well, maybe I do but it's for your own good. I just don't like to see you working so hard.'

'And now I won't have to. I have something else to think about, don't I?'

Reaching up, she kissed him on the mouth then stepped back before he could return the favour. 'Naughty, naughty,' she said, wagging her finger at him. 'Don't forget that you promised to be a model of decorum.'

She gave him a teasing smile then whisked out of the staff-room, leaving him with some very un-decorous thoughts! Lewis sighed as he headed for his room because it wasn't going to be easy to keep this up. He wanted Helen so much but he couldn't do anything about it until he was sure about the effect it would have on Kristy if he introduced her into their lives. Maybe his daughter would accept her, but maybe she wouldn't, and the thought left him teetering on the brink of despair.

He couldn't bear to imagine a future without Helen.

CHAPTER TWELVE

THE following weeks were the happiest of Helen's entire life. Even though she and Lewis could only snatch the odd moment together, it was worth it.

They fell into the habit of arriving a bit earlier each day so they could have coffee together before they started work. Ten minutes might not have seemed very much to some people but the time was precious to her.

One day she packed a picnic and met him at lunchtime before he set off to do the house calls. It was a perfect spring day so they found a quiet spot in the woods just outside the town. And after they'd eaten their lunch they made love under the canopy of trees. Helen knew that she was falling in love with him but she didn't tell him that because she didn't want to put any pressure on him. However, when he asked her if she would like to watch Kristy riding the following Saturday, she couldn't help hoping that the situation would grow easier in time. She just had to be patient a little while longer.

Her happiness soon spilt over into her work and she began to make some changes to how the surgery was run. Janet and Eve were encouraged to be extra-vigilant when making appointments. There was a bit of grumbling at first but the patients soon accepted that they didn't always need to see a doctor for minor ailments. She also advertised for a practice manager and just a few days after the woman started work, Helen was enjoying the benefits of having someone else to do all the paperwork.

She also decided to give Amy extra responsibility by appointing her as their first nurse-practitioner. Because they were seeing fewer patients each day, Amy was able to take time off for the extra training that was needed. Amy was thrilled by her promotion and Helen was sure it had been the right thing to do.

Even Harry seemed to be inspired by the new, less pressurised system. The week before his contract was due to expire, he asked if he could stay on, an offer which Helen gratefully accepted. Everyone seemed happier, in fact, and it just strengthened the feeling she had that things were going to work out in the end for her and Lewis. She seemed to float through the days on a cloud of newly discovered optimism until the bubble burst one morning when she woke up and was violently sick. As she left the bathroom, she was struck by a thought so shocking that she had to sit down on the stairs as her legs buckled. It had been six weeks since she'd last had a period so was it possible that she was pregnant?

Panic welled up inside her as she considered the idea. She wasn't on the Pill, and she and Lewis hadn't used any other form of contraception so she definitely couldn't rule out the possibility and she didn't know what she was going to do if it was true. Lewis had made it perfectly clear that he couldn't make any sort of commitment while he had Kristy to consider, so how would he feel about her having a baby? Would he be upset about the added responsibility of another child?

Then there was the effect it might have on Kristy if she was presented with a new baby brother or sister. Her life had been turned upside down once already, and a new sibling might be too much for her to deal with. A lot of children were jealous when a new baby came onto the scene, and Kristy might resent having to share her father with another child when she had only just got to know him. The thought that it might cause untold damage to Lewis's relationship with his daughter was more than Helen could bear. Tears streamed down her face because this should have been the happiest moment of her life and it had turned into a nightmare!

Lewis found it incredibly difficult not to show how he felt about Helen whenever they were together, but he knew that he had to be sensible. So far they had avoided any gossip in the surgery and he didn't want to rock the boat. It wouldn't be right to start any rumours flying around the town when he might not be able to make that final commitment to her.

Granted, his relationship with Kristy seemed to be improving almost daily, but she was still very vulnerable. Although she seemed to like Helen, introducing Helen into her life on a permanent basis was a big step and he didn't want to rush things. He needed to bide his time even though he couldn't help feeling impatient about the restrictions he'd imposed on them. He wanted to be with Helen every minute of every day, not just snatch the odd minute in between seeing patients!

He went to work even earlier than usual the following day in the hope that he could spend some extra time with Helen before the others arrived. However, when he tried the door, he discovered it was locked. He frowned as he took out his keys because it wasn't like Helen to be late. In the three months he'd been working there, she had been the first to arrive each day and he couldn't help worrying what had happened to her.

He told himself he was being silly as he brought in the post but when she still hadn't arrived by the time they were due to open, he was really concerned. He was just about to phone her home when she came in and his heart sank when he saw how pale she looked.

'Are you OK?' he asked, hurrying over to her.

'I'm fine.' She gave him a cool little smile. 'I didn't hear my alarm going off and overslept.'

'Easily done,' he said lightly, wondering if it was his imagination or if she really was being rather distant towards him that morning. He glanced round when Harry suddenly appeared, wishing that they hadn't been interrupted because he wanted to ask her what was wrong.

'So you've made it at last, have you, Helen?' the locum observed with a grin. 'Maybe you should give up the nights out? You can't keep burning the candle at both ends, you know!'

'Thank you, Harry. I shall bear it in mind.'

She excused herself before Lewis could say anything. He watched her go with a frown on his face. Had she been out last night and was that why she'd not heard her alarm ringing? He turned to Harry, wondering if the locum knew something he didn't.

'What was that about Helen burning the candle at both ends? Did she go somewhere special last night?'

'I've no idea.' Harry grinned. 'I was just joking, although now that you mention it, she didn't deny it, did she? Maybe she had a date and that's why she couldn't drag herself out of bed this morning.'

'*A date*,' Lewis repeated, totally stunned by the suggestion.

'Uh-huh. There's no reason why she shouldn't go out and have fun, is there? And you have to admit that she's been looking very chirpy recently,' the locum added, warming to the subject. 'Maybe that guy she saw a few weeks ago is still on the scene?'

'John Dancer, you mean?' Lewis shook his head. 'I don't think so.'

'Why not? Helen's a good-looking woman and it would be very strange if she didn't have someone waiting in the wings.'

Harry didn't say anything else. He went back to his room, leaving Lewis mulling over what he'd heard. He didn't really believe that Helen was seeing someone else, of course. He would have known if she was...

Wouldn't he?

Fear rose sickly inside him as the first tiny doubt blossomed into a bigger one. He had no idea what Helen did when they weren't together. She could be seeing someone else and she had every right to do so, too. After all, she hadn't made him any promises, just as he hadn't made any to her. Just because he didn't want to be with anyone else, it didn't mean she felt the same way. She could have been out with John last night, or any other man of her choosing. And there wasn't a thing he could do about it!

Helen's hands were trembling as she opened her bag and took out the pregnancy testing kit which she'd bought on her way to work. She'd had to drive to the next town to buy it because she couldn't risk anyone seeing her in the local chemist's shop. She read the instructions on the box then slipped it into her pocket and went to the bathroom. There were patients arriving but she couldn't wait to find out if her suspicion was correct.

Five minutes later she had her answer and her heart began to pound as she stared at the two blue lines that had appeared in the window of the device. Although the manufacturers had stated that no test was completely accurate, she knew the statistics: urine tests were ninety-seven per cent accurate if they returned a positive result so there was no doubt in her mind that she was having a baby.

She dropped the kit into the bin and washed her hands, trying to quell the feeling of panic that threatened to overwhelm her. She'd never given any thought to the fact that she might fall pregnant and now she would have to deal with the consequences of her actions because there would be consequences, and not just for her either. This would affect Lewis, too, and it made it doubly difficult to decide what to do: either she kept the baby or she had a termination.

Her mind immediately recoiled. Even though she knew all the reasons why she shouldn't have a baby, she couldn't get rid of it. Having a child of her own had been her dream for so long and this might be her only chance to make it come true. She couldn't just destroy this precious life that was growing inside her because it wasn't convenient. She would have to tell Lewis that she was pregnant. They had made this baby together and they would deal with the situation together.

It was a relief to have reached a decision, even though she knew she wouldn't relax until she'd spoken to him. She worked through her morning list in record time, anxious to see him before he left to do the home visits. She had an antenatal clinic that afternoon so she couldn't arrange to meet him outside the surgery, as she would have preferred to do. She would have to tell him her news here and hope it wasn't too great a shock for him.

She opened her door so that she would see him when he left his room. As soon as she heard his voice, she jumped up, waiting impatiently while he had a last word with his patient. It was Lucy Maguire and Helen was pleased to hear the girl sounding more like her usual self.

'Thanks again, Dr Cole. I'll make sure Josh finishes the medicine you've given him.'

'It's very important that he does. We don't want you worrying your mum again, do we, Josh?'

'I wish!' Lucy laughed. 'I spend my life worrying about him and his brother. I don't blame you for just having one child— it's double the work and double the worry when you have two!'

'One's more than enough for me,' he said lightly. 'I love Kristy to pieces but I'm certainly not planning on adding to my family. I'm not that much of a masochist!'

Lucy laughed but Helen couldn't find anything amusing about the comment. Lewis didn't want any more children and he couldn't have made that any clearer. It made her see what a mistake it would be to tell him that she was pregnant. He wouldn't welcome the news because he didn't want another child. He had his daughter and his family was complete. It was the same situation all over again, the one she'd been through before with Ian, only this time it was far worse. This time she was *having* a baby, and Lewis wouldn't want it.

She closed the door and sat down at her desk. Her head was spinning but she had to work out what she was going to do. She wasn't going to abort her child so she would have to leave Summerfield, and that way nobody would need to know that she was pregnant.

She would have to sell The Beeches, of course—she would need the money from the sale to support herself until the baby was old enough for her to return to work. But she wouldn't sell the house. It was Tom and Katie's home and she wanted them to have it as an investment for their future.

Helen took a deep breath, her decision made. She would start again in a new town where nobody knew her—just her and her baby. It might not be the way she'd envisaged having a child but she would make it work. And having Lewis's son or daughter to care for would help to make up for the fact that she could never have him.

Tears sprang to her eyes but there was no point lying to herself. She loved Lewis with all her heart. He might not have room in his life for her and their child, but it didn't change how she felt about him. She placed her hand on her tummy. Their precious child was going to be the centre of her world from now on.

The lunch-break flew past so that it was time for the antenatal clinic before Helen had a chance to draw breath. Lisa Pendleton was due for a check-up again that day and she arrived, huffing and puffing and generally out of sorts. Thankfully, she'd given up the idea of having a termination after her boyfriend had threatened to leave her if she got rid of the baby, but she still had a litany of complaints, which Helen listened to with a little more sympathy that day. In a few months' time it might be her complaining about heartburn and running to the loo all the time!

'My ankles are all puffy, too. They're like an elephant's!'

Helen stooped down and examined the girl's ankles, gently pressing the swollen skin. 'You do seem to have a lot of fluid around your ankles, Lisa. Have you been resting enough? You need to take life a bit easier now you're in the third trimester of your pregnancy.'

'I'm fed up with sitting at home every night,' Lisa declared mutinously. 'I need to go out and have some fun sometimes.'

'I'm not suggesting that you sit at home every night until your baby is born, but you do need to take care of yourself.' Helen fetched the sphygmomanometer and placed it on the desk so she could check Lisa's blood pressure. 'You're still working so that means you're already putting an extra strain on your body. Making sure that you rest at night would make a big difference.'

'I only went to the pub to meet my friends,' Lisa protested. 'They wanted me to go with them to a club but I was too tired. I was back home by midnight.'

'I see. Well, just do your best to take life a little easier, won't you?' Helen wrapped the cuff around the girl's arm and inflated it. She frowned when she saw the reading. 'Your blood pressure is slightly higher than it should be so I'd like you to give me a urine sample before you leave. Have you been suffering any headaches recently or noticed any kind of visual disturbance?'

'No, nothing like that.'

'And you haven't been vomiting or feeling nauseous?'

'No. Why are you asking me all these questions, Dr Daniels? Is there something wrong with me?'

'I'm just being extra-careful,' she explained soothingly. 'There could be a simple explanation why your ankles are swollen or it could be an indication of something more serious. I need to find out which it is.'

'What do you mean by serious?' Lisa asked anxiously.

'Pre-eclampsia affects about seven per cent of all pregnant women. It can be very mild or it can develop into something far more dangerous, which can place the mother and the child at risk. I just want to rule it out in your case.'

'My aunt had pre-eclampsia,' Lisa exclaimed. 'She was really ill, too. She had some sort of a fit and we didn't think she was going to pull through.'

'It's eclampsia when it reaches that stage,' Helen corrected. 'Pre-eclampsia isn't as severe but it's seen as a warning of what could happen. The combination of high blood pressure, protein in the urine and oedema—that's fluid in the tissues—are all indications of pre-eclampsia, so that's why I want to monitor you very carefully for the next few weeks.'

'And you think it would help if I got more rest?' Lisa queried.

'I do. You work in the florist's and that means you're on your feet all day. It would make sense if you tried to rest on an evening.'

'I certainly don't want to be as ill as my aunt was,' Lisa declared. 'I'll just have to take your advice, I suppose, and not go out so much.'

'There's no reason why you can't go out at the weekend when you're not working. And your friends can always visit you at home,' Helen said encouragingly.

Lisa left a few minutes later after promising to provide a urine sample on her way out. She seemed far more resolute about her pregnancy than she'd been in the past and Helen was quietly hopeful that they'd turned a corner. However, as she went to call in her next patient, she realised that very soon she would be in need of antenatal care, too. She could sign on at a practice in a neighbouring town, but news of her visits was bound to leak out. If she hoped to avoid people finding out about the baby, she would have to put her plans into action and leave Summerfield as soon as possible. It was going to be a big upheaval, but this baby she was carrying was her main concern now. She was going to do everything in her power to make sure it was safe and happy.

'You're *leaving* Summerfield?'

Lewis couldn't have been more shocked if Helen had announced that she was flying to the moon. When she'd waylaid him after he'd come back from doing the calls and had told him that she was calling a staff meeting that night, he'd never envisaged that this was the reason for it.

He glanced at Harry and Amy but they seemed just as shocked as him so obviously they hadn't suspected what was going on.

'But why are you leaving?' he demanded. 'I thought you loved living here.'

'I do, but I've spent the whole of my working life in this town and now I feel that I'd like a fresh challenge, which is why I'm putting the practice on the market.'

'And are you selling the house as well?' he asked, scarcely able to believe what he was hearing. Just a few weeks ago she had been clinging to the past and refusing to make even the smallest changes. Now she was selling up and moving on, and he couldn't understand why she hadn't mentioned the idea to him before.

'No. The house belongs to Tom and Katie. I know that technically Ian left it to me but I want them to have it.' She gave a little shrug. 'It's up to them if they decide to live there after they've finished their studies. In the meantime, I'm planning on renting it out. The income it generates will be paid into a trust fund for them.'

'You seem to have everything all worked out,' he observed quietly, thinking what a massive understatement that was. She'd covered every angle yet she hadn't hinted at her plans when they'd been together.

The thought was just too painful. He had to blot it out of his mind as she continued.

'I have. It's not been an easy decision but I'm certain it's the right one. And that's what matters most of all, isn't it?'

Lewis felt a shaft of pain run through him. He knew that she was telling him that she didn't care what he thought, and he couldn't understand what had happened to make her feel like this…unless she'd grown tired of always being on the sidelines of his life. What woman would be happy to settle for what he was able to offer her? Especially if there was someone else willing to make the kind of commitment he couldn't?

The thought was too much on top of everything else. Lewis found it difficult not to show how devastated he felt by the idea. 'So how far along are you with your plans? Obviously, it will affect us all if you sell the practice so I hope you will take that into account.'

'Of course. I shall be advertising the sale in all the usual journals at the end of this month. I can't see that there will be a problem finding a buyer—there was a lot of interest when I advertised your post. And, naturally, I shall include you in any decisions I make. I'd also like to give you first option to purchase the practice if you're interested.'

'Thank you.' Lewis did his best to behave in a suitable fashion, but he felt physically sick when he realised how much thought she'd put into this. It wasn't some spur-of-the-moment decision but a carefully considered plan for the future. He couldn't believe how painful it was to know that she'd cut him out so completely.

He quickly excused himself and went to the staffroom, hoping a cup of coffee would help him pull himself together. Harry and Amy must have had the same idea because they arrived a few minutes later.

'Well, that was a shock!' Harry declared, flopping down into a chair. 'I *never* thought Helen would sell up and leave, did you, Amy?'

'Never in a million years.' Amy suddenly sighed. 'Although maybe I should have realised it could happen when I heard about Dr Dancer leaving.'

'What do you mean?' Lewis demanded.

'Apparently he's moving to America. He's been appointed head of a brand-new unit that's just opened in Boston. My friend Kelly works in the gastroenterology unit, and they're all gutted about it… Oops, sorry! The pun was unintentional.'

'And you think that's why Helen is selling up?' Lewis ignored Harry's chortle of laughter. 'Because she's going with him?'

'What other reason can you think of?' Amy shrugged as she spooned instant coffee into their mugs. 'All right, so Helen has never mentioned a word about Dr Dancer since they went out that night, but she's definitely been acting differently recently.

All the changes she's made and now this… I mean, why else would she suddenly decide to sell up? No, I think she's going with him and that's why she's so keen to get rid of this place all of a sudden.'

'It does make sense,' he agreed, trying not to let her see how wretched he felt. He didn't want to believe that Helen was leaving to be with another man, but what other reason could she have for making such a life-changing decision? Sickness welled up inside him and he strode to the door, terrified that he was going to make a fool of himself if he stayed there.

'What about your coffee?' Amy called after him, but he didn't answer. He couldn't when he was trying so desperately hard not to break down.

He went back to his room and grabbed his case. He had to collect Kristy from the after-school club and he was determined to be in control of himself when he got there. Kristy was the only person who mattered now—her happiness was his sole concern. If he repeated the mantra often enough then maybe he'd forget about Helen and this agony he felt.

He unlocked the car and took a deep breath. Helen was going to build a new life for herself and there was no point wishing there was a place in it for him and Kristy.

CHAPTER THIRTEEN

HELEN felt as though she was tiptoeing over eggshells in the days following her announcement. The atmosphere in the surgery grew increasingly tense because of the uncertainty about what might happen in the future. She felt terribly guilty about letting everyone down but she didn't have a choice.

The response to her advertisement was as good as she'd hoped it would be. There were a lot of people interested in buying the premises, as well as her share of the business. She organised the interviews and gave Lewis a list of everyone she intended to see. She had hoped that he would take her up on her offer to give him first refusal, but he remained very tight-lipped about what was happening. She could only assume that he didn't want to take on the responsibilities of senior partner because of his commitment to Kristy, and it was painful to know that the child she was carrying would never benefit from such devotion.

On a personal level, Lewis made no secret of the fact that he didn't want anything to do with her. If she walked into a room, he walked out. There were no more early morning cups of coffee, no picnics in the woods, no contact at all beyond the basics, and she missed him unbearably even though she understood why he was behaving that way. He was hurt and offended because she hadn't told him what she was planning to do, and there was nothing she could do about it. She couldn't tell him the truth about why she was leaving when she had to protect her unborn child.

Most days Lewis felt as though he was going crazy. Trying to maintain a professional front at work became increasingly difficult when every day that passed brought the day when Helen would leave that bit closer. He longed to beg her not to go but knew that she wouldn't listen to him. Why should she? She was following her heart and he had no right to spoil things for her.

The stress of keeping his silence started to show and he became increasingly tetchy. He even found himself snapping at Kristy over breakfast one morning—something he bitterly regretted when he saw how upset she was. He tried to smooth things over as he drove her to school but she was unusually quiet—just like she'd been when he'd brought her back to England. As he kissed her goodbye, he promised himself that he would never let his feelings get the better of him again. Maybe it did feel as though the bottom had fallen out of his world, but it wasn't fair to take his unhappiness out on his daughter.

His spirits had fallen to an all-time low by the time he arrived at the surgery, and it didn't help that the first person he saw was Helen herself. She was sorting through the post, and she looked so sad that he was instantly alarmed. Wasn't she as confident about this move as she tried to appear?

His heart started to pound as he hurried towards her. He knew how foolish it was to hope that she might change her mind but he couldn't help it. If there was any doubt in her mind about what she was doing then she mustn't go through with it: he wouldn't let her!

'Are you OK?' he said softly, stopping beside her.

'Of course.' She gave him a smile that didn't quite reach her eyes.

'Are you sure?' He touched her arm, feeling the current that shot through his fingers when his skin made contact with hers. It was such a long time since he'd touched her, held her, kissed and caressed her that he was like a starving man. Even these crumbs—the barest touch of skin on skin—tasted like heaven. It took a huge effort of will not to haul her into his arms and beg her not to leave him.

'Of course I'm sure!' She jerked her arm away but he could see the pain in her eyes and it worried him even more.

'Giving up your job and your home is a big decision, Helen. You need to be absolutely certain that you aren't going to regret it.'

'What I choose to do is my business. It has nothing to do with you or anyone else.'

'Is that a fact?' he said sceptically, and she frowned.

'Yes, it is.'

'Really? So it doesn't have anything to do with John Dancer, then?'

'John,' she repeated, as though she had no idea to who he was talking about. The thought that she was going to try and fob him off after what they'd been to one another was more than he could stand and he rounded on her.

'Oh, come on, Helen! Everyone knows what's going on. John is moving to Boston to take up a new post and you're going with him.' He laughed harshly, anger and frustration spilling over. 'I don't know why you're being so secretive. You're a free agent and you don't owe an allegiance to anyone—least of all to me!'

'But I'm not—'

'Morning!'

Helen stopped abruptly when Harry appeared. When the locum came over and asked Lewis if he'd look at some test results that had arrived the previous night, she excused herself and went to her room. Dropping the bundle of letters she was holding onto her desk, she went to the window and stared out. *Lewis believed that she was leaving because of John Dancer?*

Hearing that had been a big enough shock, but an even bigger one had been the look on his face. He'd looked…tortured. So stricken, in fact, that it was as though his heart was being ripped apart. Was it possible that he loved her as much as she loved him?

The thought filled her with elation. She wanted to rush straight back and demand that he tell her the truth, but was it the right thing to do? If he felt that strongly about her, why hadn't he told her so before? Had he been afraid to admit to his feelings because of the impact it could have on Kristy?

Her heart sank because she knew it was true. Lewis was desperate to protect his daughter and that was why he'd been so careful to keep their affair a secret. If she forced him to admit how he felt, it wouldn't help. It would put him under even more pressure and that was before he found out about the baby she was carrying! How could she demand an answer when it might create the very problems he wanted to avoid?

Helen's eyes misted with tears. She knew that she would never do anything to hurt him. She loved him far too much. It would be better to let him think that she was planning to spend her life with another man than cause him such heartache.

The day was the worst Lewis could remember. He was bitterly aware that he'd made a fool of himself by letting Helen see how he felt about her. She knew now that he loved her and there wasn't a thing he could do about it. If she asked him how he felt, he would have to tell her the truth but, as the morning wore on, the likelihood of that happening became increasingly remote and that upset him even more. She didn't intend to ask him because she wasn't interested.

Thankfully, it was his afternoon off so he left as soon as surgery ended. He still hadn't got round to changing his car so he decided he might as well do it that day instead of putting it off any longer. He'd just reached the car showroom when his mobile phone rang so he pulled into a parking bay, sighing when he saw that the call was from the surgery. He could have done with a couple of hours to himself before he had to think about work again.

'Lewis Cole.'

'It's me—Helen.'

Lewis's heart jolted when he heard her voice. He could feel the blood roaring through his veins, melting away the chill that had enveloped him since that morning. Had she phoned to tell him that she *wasn't* leaving, that she *couldn't* leave because she loved him?

'I'm sorry, Lewis, but there's no easy way to tell you this. Kristy is missing.'

'Missing?' he repeated numbly.

'Yes. The headmistress just phoned the surgery so I'm passing on the message. They've searched the school and there's no sign of her. They thought maybe you'd collected her at lunchtime—'

'No! Why would I? There's no reason to take her out of school.'

Lewis could hear the panic in his voice but he didn't care. His daughter was missing and nobody knew where she'd gone!

'Then you'd better phone the school and tell the headmistress that.' Helen's tone was firm. 'I'll get on to the police. We can't afford to delay in a situation like this.'

'No, of course not.' He could feel himself trembling as he tried to punch in the number for the school. He suddenly realised that he hadn't ended this call yet. 'I'll have to go,' he said, his voice grating with fear.

'Of course. I take it that you'll be going straight to the school?'

'Yes.'

'I'll meet you there.'

She hung up before he could reply, but he was in no frame of mind to wonder why she'd offered to meet him. He phoned the school and was put straight through to the headmistress who explained that Kristy hadn't been seen since lunchtime.

Lewis brusquely informed her that he would go straight there and cut the connection while she was explaining that nothing like this had happened before. He didn't give a damn about the school's safety record. He only cared about his daughter and the fact that nobody knew where she was.

He broke all records getting to the school but Helen was already there when he arrived. She jumped out of her car and hurried over to him.

'The police are on their way. They should be here within the next ten minutes or so.'

'Are any of the other children missing?' he demanded as he strode into the playground.

'The head didn't mention that. But she was very flustered when I spoke to her.'

'And so she should be,' he said grimly. He went straight to the headmistress's study once they were inside and flung open the door without bothering to knock. There wasn't time for social niceties when his daughter was missing.

'Dr Cole!' the woman exclaimed, leaping to her feet.

'Are any of the other children missing?' he demanded. Where had Kristy gone? And had she left of her own accord or had someone taken her? The thought made him feel so ill that it was difficult to breathe.

'No. It's just Kristy who's missing. I really don't know how it happened. We keep the gates locked during the day so it isn't as though the children can just wander out whenever they choose.'

'And nobody can wander in either?' he said shortly, and saw her blanch.

'No, no! We have staff on duty and they're very vigilant... Or they are normally,' she added uncertainly.

'Maybe we could speak to some of Kristy's friends,' Helen suggested, and he was grateful to her for remaining so calm when he couldn't.

'Of course! An excellent idea, Dr Daniels. I'll take you straight through to her classroom so you can speak to her teacher.'

The headmistress led them out of the room, obviously relieved to be able to do something to help. Lewis followed her, trying to contain the fear that was twisting his guts. Anything could have happened to Kristy; anyone could have taken her. The thought was more than he could bear.

'She'll be all right, Lewis. We'll find her.' Helen slipped her hand into his and squeezed it.

'I hope you're right. I don't know what I'll do if anything has happened to her...' He couldn't go on. The lump in his throat was so enormous that the words couldn't get past it, but she understood.

She squeezed his hand again and held onto it as they made their way to the classroom. Lewis couldn't begin to explain what a comfort it was to have her there with him and didn't try. All he knew was that he needed her at that moment more than he'd needed anyone in his entire life.

The headmistress knocked on the door then hurried into the room. They followed her, standing to one side while she spoke to the teacher. Lewis tried to curb his impatience as the two women conferred. Didn't they realise how urgent the situation was and that every second wasted placed his daughter in even greater danger? Finally—when he thought he couldn't wait any longer—the teacher beckoned to a boy sitting by the window.

'This is Danny Appleton,' she explained as the child came over to them. 'He's Kristy's best friend—isn't that right, Danny?'

The boy didn't reply but Lewis had seen the guilty look Danny had given them and his heart surged. If he wasn't mistaken, Danny knew something about Kristy's disappearance, although he sensed it wouldn't be easy to get the information out of him.

Bending down, he looked into the little boy's eyes. 'Do you know where Kristy has gone, Danny?'

Danny shook his head, but Lewis was more convinced than ever that the boy knew something. He smiled at him, doing his best to project a reassuring front.

'It's very important that you tell me the truth, Danny. I promise you that you won't get into trouble if you tell me where Kristy has gone.'

Once again the boy shook his head and Lewis found it hard to contain his frustration. However, before he could say anything, Helen forestalled him.

Bending down, she put her arm round the little boy's shoulders. 'Do you remember when Charlie, your dog, got lost and you were really upset, Danny?'

Once again the boy nodded, his eyes locked on Helen's face, and she smiled at him. 'He was such a silly dog, wasn't he? He ran off when you were playing ball then couldn't find his way home. Well, Dr Cole is afraid that Kristy won't be able to find her way home, too, so that's why he needs to know where she is.'

'I promised I wouldn't tell anyone,' Danny muttered.

'And it's important to keep a promise.' Helen nodded. 'I understand that, Danny, because once you've given your word, you should stick to it. But it's different in this case. Kristy could get hurt if she's wandering about on her own. She doesn't know the town like you do, and she might not be able to find her way back home. I think it would be OK if you broke your promise just this once because you're trying to help her.'

Danny bit his lip. It was obvious that he was trying to decide what he should do. Lewis held his breath, knowing that he didn't dare say anything in case he frightened the boy.

'She's gone to the old tannery,' Danny blurted out. 'She said that she didn't want to go home in case her dad shouted at her again.'

Lewis felt his insides twist in agony. This was all *his* fault! He'd been snappy with Kristy that morning and that's why she'd run away.

He didn't say a word as Helen thanked the boy and quickly led the way from the classroom. He heard the headmistress say something about them waiting for the police to arrive and Helen replied that they wouldn't wait but would drive straight to the tannery, but he didn't utter a word. How could he? He had scared his own daughter into running away and he didn't think he would ever forgive himself for what he'd done.

Somehow he found himself in Helen's car. His mind was awash with pain so that he was on autopilot. Helen glanced at him as she started the engine. 'Fasten your seat belt.'

Lewis buckled up, feeling the full weight of his misery wash over him. What kind of man was he that he could hurt the people he loved most in the world?

'She'll be all right, Lewis. You just need to have faith. We'll find her. I promise you.'

The gentleness in Helen's voice was too much. Tears sprang to his eyes and he didn't even bother trying to hide them from her. 'She ran away because of me, because I was snappy with her this morning and scared her.'

'It's not easy being a parent so don't be too hard on yourself. You're just a normal human being, Lewis, not a saint. You can't be perfect all the time.'

She tried to tease him into a smile but it didn't work. He knew what he was and that what had happened would haunt him until his dying day.

'I should have been more sensitive. I know how vulnerable Kristy is and I shouldn't have been so sharp with her. She's only a child and I should have made allowances for her!'

'Why were you annoyed with her?' Helen paused at the junction and glanced at him. 'Had she done something naughty?'

'Not really. It was me. I've been feeling very edgy recently and I allowed my feelings to get the better of me.'

'Was it because of what's been happening at work? Your edginess, I mean.'

'Yes. It was a shock to hear that you were leaving, Helen.'

'I was trying to do what was best. For everyone,' she added cryptically.

Lewis wasn't sure what she meant and before he could ask, he spotted the tannery up ahead. He leant forward as she drew up in the gateway. There was no sign of Kristy and his heart plummeted because he had no idea what he was going to do if she wasn't here.

'Let's take a look inside.' Helen opened the car door and got out. Lewis got out as well and hurried to the gate. It was padlocked and didn't look as though it had been opened for some time, but there was a gap in the hedge through which they could squeeze.

He climbed through then helped Helen after him and looked around. There were a lot of buildings in the compound and most of them were in a very poor state of repair. 'Let's try over there first.' He pointed to the smallest of the outbuildings.

'Why don't we split up? That way we can cover more ground.'

'Fair enough. But be careful, won't you? Some of that brickwork looks very unsafe.'

'Don't worry about me,' she said lightly, and he knew that he couldn't let it pass. Even though he was desperately worried about his daughter, he couldn't keep up this pretence of indifference.

'I'll always worry about you, Helen. I can't help it.' He touched her gently on the cheek then turned away because this was neither the time nor the place to say anything else. Maybe there never would be a right time but he couldn't worry about it now when Kristy needed him.

He ran over to the outhouse and opened the rickety old door, but there was no sign of his daughter. He tried one of the sheds next and drew another blank. It was the same in the next few buildings he checked. Hope was fading fast when he forced open the door to one of the warehouses so that when he spotted the little girl, curled up on a pile of old sacks, he could scarcely believe his eyes.

Lewis ran across the concrete floor and knelt down beside her, his heart welling with emotion when he realised that she was fast asleep. Reaching out, he smoothed a dark curl off her cheek, feeling the intensity of his love for her overwhelm him.

'Daddy...' Her eyes slowly opened and he smiled at her.

'Hi! I've come to take you home, poppet. I'm sorry if I scared you this morning when I shouted at you. I didn't mean to.'

'I thought you didn't love me any more,' she whispered. 'Joe used to shout at me when Mommy went away. He said I was a pest and that he was tired of looking after me.' Her eyes suddenly filled with tears. 'That's why Mommy didn't come back, isn't it? Because I was naughty and she didn't love me any more?'

'No! That isn't true and Joe should *never* have told you that.' It was all Lewis could do to remain calm. He couldn't believe that anyone could be so cruel as to have said that to a child. Taking hold of her hands, he held them tightly in both of his.

'Your Mommy loved you very much, sweetheart. She didn't care if you were naughty sometimes because she would never have stopped loving you. She didn't want to leave you but she was hurt very badly in the accident and she died and went to heaven. That's why she didn't come back—not because of anything you did.'

'And you don't think I'm a pest, too?' she whispered.

'No, I don't. You are my precious little girl and I'll always love you no matter what happens.'

'And you won't go away, like Joe did?'

'No, I shall never go away and leave you. You're my own, special little girl and I love you very much. I'm going to take care of you until you're all grown up, and even then I'll still be there whenever you need me. I love you, Kristy, and nothing you do will make me stop loving you.'

He picked her up in his arms and held her close. 'And I shall never let anything bad happen to you ever again.'

'I love you, too, Daddy,' she murmured, snuggling against him.

'And I love you, sweetheart,' he replied thickly, overcome by emotion. He carried her outside, smiling when he spotted Helen coming out of a building close to where he was standing. 'Look who I've found.'

'Kristy!'

She came rushing over, her beautiful face alight with pleasure, and he responded instinctively. Bending down, he kissed
her on the mouth and felt his heart jerk in delight when she kissed
him back. He drew back and looked at her because there was no
point trying to hide how he felt when his feelings must have been
etched all over his face.

'I love you, Helen. Maybe I shouldn't say this but I need to
tell you the truth. I love you and I always shall.'

Tears welled to her eyes as she put her arms around both him
and Kristy. 'I love you, too. I can't believe how stupid we've been
these past few weeks.'

'Neither can I.'

One more too-brief kiss then, all of a sudden the police arrived. By the time he'd explained that Kristy was fine and the
crisis was over, there was no opportunity to say anything else.
He assured the officer in charge that he would call at the police station to give a statement then followed Helen to the car.
She opened the back door while he strapped Kristy into the rear
seat. The little girl was worn out after her ordeal and soon fell
asleep. She was still asleep when they drew up in front of his
house so he dug his keys out of his pocket and handed them
to Helen.

'Can you open the door while I carry her inside? I think it
would be best if I took her straight up to bed, don't you?'

'I do. The poor little mite is exhausted.'

Helen shot a loving look at the little girl and his heart swelled
with joy because there was no way that she could have feigned
such feelings. Leaning over, he kissed her on the mouth, letting
his lips linger in the place where they had longed to be these past
weeks. The kiss wasn't without passion but the most wonderful
thing about it was its healing qualities. It felt as though all the
pain that he'd stored up had melted away and he couldn't believe
how much better he felt when they drew apart.

'I needed that,' he said roughly.

'Me, too.' She smiled at him, her face alight with love. 'I've missed you, Lewis. Having to pretend that I didn't care has been a nightmare.'

'Is that why you decided to sell up and leave?'

'Partly.'

A shadow crossed her face and he felt a chill invade him as he realised that he had overlooked one very important issue. Helen had said that she loved him, and he believed her, but where did John Dancer fit into this scenario?

'Daddy?'

He glanced round when Kristy suddenly woke up. 'I'm right here, darling,' he said quickly, when he saw the panic on her face.

'I'll open the door for you,' Helen said hurriedly as she got out of the car.

Lewis followed more slowly, wondering what was going on. On the one hand she claimed to love him yet on the other she'd been about to embark on a new life with another man. It didn't make sense. He tried to put aside his fear as he lifted Kristy out of the car. The nap seemed to have done her good—she insisted on walking up the path and told him that she was hungry once they were inside. He sent her upstairs to wash her hands, although he wasn't overly concerned about the matter of hygiene. However, he needed to speak to Helen on her own. They had to settle this issue before they could do anything else, but she forestalled him.

'You need to look after Kristy so I'll leave you to it. Don't worry about surgery tonight. Harry and I will split your list between us.' She hurried to the door but he refused to let her leave without making some attempt to sort things out.

'We need to talk, Helen.'

'I know. But not now.' She summoned a smile but he could see the fear in her eyes and it scared him. Why was she so afraid? Because she was worried about hurting him? It took him all his time not to demand an answer but he could hear Kristy coming back down the stairs.

'When, then?'

'Tonight. After I finish work.' Another brief smile then she was gone.

Lewis took a deep breath then smiled as his daughter came skipping into the kitchen, but it was all a front. Inside, he was filled with dread. He really didn't know how he was going to bear it if he lost Helen now.

CHAPTER FOURTEEN

HELEN went straight back to the surgery and broke the good news. Everyone was deeply relieved that Kristy had been found, safe and well. She had a word with Harry and explained that they would have to cover for Lewis that evening then went to her room, needing some time on her own. Part of her was so elated by Lewis's declaration of love that she wanted to rush out and tell everyone. However, the more cautious side warned her it could be a mistake. Maybe he did love her but how would he feel when he found out she was pregnant?

It was bound to have an effect on his relationship with Kristy so would he welcome the news? Or would he be so horrified at the thought of her having his child that it would affect his feelings for her? She had no idea how he would react, which made it all the more difficult to know what to do. Should she tell him tonight, or should she keep it a secret? But if she didn't tell him, she would have to leave Summerfield because he would soon find out.

By the time surgery ended, Helen was no nearer to making a decision. She knew that she couldn't risk going to see Lewis while she was in that state so she went home. He would wonder where she was, but eventually he would come up with an explanation, even if it wasn't the right one. And maybe it would be easier for them both if he did—less stressful for her not to have to lie to him, and less traumatic for him not to have to listen. She would let him draw his own conclusions because in the end it might be the kindest thing to do.

Seven o'clock came and went and there was still no sign of Helen. Lewis phoned the surgery but hung up when his call was diverted to the answering service. Where was she? he thought as he paced the sitting-room floor. She'd said she would come back that night so why wasn't she here? Didn't she know how important it was that they should clear up all the misunderstandings? Or was there nothing to clear up? Maybe she'd had second thoughts and realised that she wasn't in love with him. If that was the case then he was better off without her!

Buoyed up by indignation, he went into the kitchen and made himself something to eat, but after just one mouthful he realised he was wasting his time. He was too emotionally gutted to worry about food. He loved Helen and she'd claimed to love him, so what the hell was going on?

Leaving his plate on the table, he stormed out of the room. Kristy was fast asleep and he hated to wake her but there was no way that he was going to leave her with a sitter after what had happened that day. He wrapped her in a blanket and carried her downstairs. She was still half-asleep when he popped her into the car and fastened her seat belt.

'Where are we going, Daddy?' she murmured sleepily.

'To see Helen, sweetheart.'

'I like Helen,' she whispered as her eyelids started to droop.

'So do I,' he muttered grimly, closing the car door. He drove straight to Helen's house and pulled into the drive. Turning off the engine, he sat for a moment while he geared himself up for what might happen. Helen might tell him to go away, or she might welcome him with open arms and an open heart, and he had to be prepared for either eventuality. However, if there was a chance that he could sort out this mess, he wasn't going to let anything get in his way!

He got out of the car and lifted Kristy off the passenger seat then knocked on the door. When Helen opened it, he didn't give her time to refuse him entry. He barged past her with his daughter in his arms and determination etched all over his face. This woman meant the whole world to him and he didn't intend to give her up without a struggle!

'Lewis! What are you doing here?'

'We need to talk.' He brushed past her and nodded towards the stairs. 'Is it all right if I put Kristy in one of the bedrooms? She's worn out after today's little episode and she needs to go to sleep.'

'I…um…' Helen took a quick breath and tried to pull herself together, but her nerves were tingling as adrenaline rushed through her veins. She had a good idea why Lewis had come, although she had no idea what she was going to say to him. 'You can put her in Katie's room. I'll show you the way.'

She hurried up the stairs, using the few seconds it took to calm herself down. Lewis couldn't force her to do anything she didn't want to do, and if she chose not to tell him about the baby that was her decision. Opening the bedroom door, she gestured towards the bed.

'She'll be fine in here. If we leave the door open, we'll be able to hear her if she wakes up.'

'Thanks.' Lewis laid his daughter on the bed and carefully tucked the blanket around her. 'I'll be downstairs if you want me, sweetheart. I'm just going to talk to Helen so you just shout out if you need me. All right?'

'A' right,' Kristy repeated sleepily, snuggling into the pillows.

Helen led the way downstairs and made straight for the sitting-room. It was a room she never used because she found the old-fashioned decor overpowering. However, it seemed fitting to take Lewis in there rather than into the less formal atmosphere of the kitchen. She needed to keep a level head and there was more likelihood of her doing that in here.

He looked around as he followed her into the room. 'This place is like a museum. It must be years since it was decorated.'

'I don't use it very often,' she said shortly, sitting down on one of the straight-backed chairs.

'I can understand why.' He sat down on the couch and stared at her. 'What's going on, Helen? You promised that you would come back to see me after evening surgery so why didn't you do so?'

'I didn't want to disturb Kristy—'

'Rubbish! It had nothing whatsoever to do with Kristy.' He leant forward and she could see the urgency in his eyes. 'I told you how I feel about you. Did it mean nothing to you?'

'Of course it meant something to me.'

'Then what's going on? Why did you run home and hide when you knew I was waiting to talk to you?' He looked down at the floor and she could see the fear in his eyes when they returned to her face. 'Did you realise that you'd got carried away in the heat of the moment and that it's not me you love?'

'There's no point talking about it,' she whispered, her voice breaking. It was so hard to hear him say such things and not be able to deny them, but she couldn't risk ruining his relationship with his daughter. 'I'm leaving Summerfield, Lewis, and you just have to accept that.'

'I don't have to accept anything! I want to know what's going on, Helen. Are you in love with me or not? It's a simple enough question so why won't you answer it?'

'Because I don't want to hurt you!' she countered, stung into replying with equal fervour.

'Hurt me? In other words, what you said to me today was a mistake.' He stood up abruptly and her heart turned over when she saw the bleakness in his eyes. It was as though every scrap of emotion had seeped from him and she couldn't believe how painful it was to see him looking that way. 'Then I'm sorry to have troubled you. I'll just fetch Kristy and leave—'

'No!' Helen didn't realise that she'd jumped up until she found herself on her feet. She gripped the back of the chair as the room started to spin. She knew that she might be making a terrible mistake, but she couldn't let him leave believing that she didn't love him. 'I didn't make a mistake. I do love you.'

'You do? Then why are you leaving Summerfield?'

'Because I have to!'

'Have to?' he repeated, frowning. 'What do you mean by that? Has Dancer got some sort of a hold over you?'

'It has nothing to do with John Dancer!' she exploded.

'But you're going to America with him, aren't you?'

'No, I'm not. I'm not sure how that rumour started but the truth is that I've not seen John since I went out for that meal with him.' She shrugged. 'He did invite me out again but I refused.'

'Why?'

'Because it wouldn't have been fair to let him think I was interested in him.'

'Then if you aren't leaving to start a new life with him, why are you going?' He took a slow step towards her then another until all of a sudden he was standing in front of her. Helen bit her lip when she saw the entreaty in his eyes. She desperately wanted to tell him the truth but how could she?

'Tell me, Helen. Please. Why are you leaving?' He touched her on the cheek and she felt the tremor that ran through his fingers as they brushed her skin. That was the moment when she knew that she was lost. How could she lie to him about something so important?

'Because I love you and I can't bear to do anything that might hurt you,' she whispered brokenly.

He closed his eyes for a moment and when he opened them again she could see the fire in their depths. 'The only thing that could hurt me is if I lost you, my darling. I love you, Helen, and I want us to be together for ever and always.'

He pulled her into his arms and cradled her against him as he dropped kisses on her hair. Helen wrapped her arms around him, needing this feeling of closeness to help her through what was to come. Maybe he did love her but she wouldn't make him choose between her and his daughter.

He kissed her softly on the mouth then let her go when she pulled back. 'There's something else, isn't there? I can tell there is. Whatever it is, we can work it out, Helen, I promise you.'

'Can we?' She gave a harsh little laugh and saw him wince.

'Yes. I love you, Helen. Nothing will change that so tell me what's wrong.'

'I'm pregnant.' The words rushed out before she could attempt to find a gentler way to tell him, and her heart contracted when she saw the shock on his face.

'Pregnant?'

'Yes. I'm sorry. I know it was stupid not to mention that I wasn't on the Pill but...'

'But it was the last thing on either of our minds,' he said with a chuckle that sent ripples through the whole of her body.

Helen stared up at him, scarcely able to believe what she was seeing. He might have looked shocked in the beginning but there was no doubt at all that he looked elated now. He pulled her back into his arms and kissed her soundly.

'It must have come as a tremendous shock to you, my love, and I'm truly sorry about that. But I'm not sorry about the baby. I can't think of anything better than us having a child together.'

'But I heard you telling Lucy Maguire that you didn't want any more children...' she began, and he groaned.

'And that's what started all this? I couldn't understand why you suddenly decided to sell up and leave when we were so happy.' He tilted her chin and looked into her eyes. 'It was just a passing comment, darling. I'd probably had a bad night...been up with Kristy because she'd had one of her nightmares...but that's all it was. I didn't really mean it.'

Tears began to stream down her cheeks when she realised that he was telling her the truth. However, despite the reassurance, maybe he didn't fully understand the problems this baby could cause.

'I'm so glad. But what about Kristy? How is she going to feel? She might be upset when she finds out that we're having a baby.

I know how difficult it's been for you to build a relationship with her and I don't want anything to come between you.'

'Nothing is going to come between us, darling. I understand now why Kristy has been so withdrawn. Tessa's boyfriend filled her head with a load of rubbish about him not wanting to look after her because she was a nuisance, and she thought that was why her mother hadn't come back. The poor little mite has been terrified of doing anything to upset me in case I didn't want her either.'

'Oh, how awful! But that makes it even more important that she knows how much you love her. She might feel jealous about having to share you with another child and I don't want her to get hurt.'

'She won't. We won't let her be hurt—you, me and this baby we're having. We'll give her all the love and stability she could possibly need.'

He took a handkerchief out of his pocket and dried her tears then kissed her again. Helen clung to him, needing the reassurance of his arms around her because she still wasn't convinced. He must have sensed that she still had reservations because he sighed as he led her to the couch.

'Let's sit down and talk about this properly. I can't think straight when I kiss you and this is one time when I need a clear head.'

She sighed wistfully as she sat down beside him. 'I knew it would cause a problem if I told you.'

'Which is why you decided to sell up and leave.' He took her hands and held them tightly. 'I'm just glad that I found out. I can't bear to imagine what might have happened if you'd gone through with your plan, my darling. I'd have lost you and our baby.'

'I'm sorry. I wasn't doing it to hurt you—just the opposite, in fact.'

'I know.' He kissed the tip of her nose, making it plain that he didn't blame her. 'We've both made mistakes. I shouldn't have made such a big thing about keeping our relationship quiet. Then you would have realised sooner how important you are to me and not had to go through all the worry of thinking you had to leave your home.'

'You did it for Kristy so don't blame yourself. And I didn't want to start any rumours flying, don't forget.' She sighed as she snuggled up against him. 'The gossips are going to have a field day when they find out.'

'Are you worried because you don't want it to seem as though you are letting Ian down in some way?' he asked gently.

'Not at all. Oh, I admit that I clung on to his ideas in the surgery for a lot longer than I should have done, but it was out of fear more than anything else. I was afraid to admit how empty my life was so I filled up the time with lots of extra jobs.' She drew back so she could look at him because she didn't want there to be any mistake about what she was saying. 'Ian was a good man and I cared about him, but I definitely never felt this way about him.'

She kissed him on the mouth, letting her actions explain how she truly felt. The kiss lasted for a long time and they were both trembling when it ended.

'I love you so much, Helen. I can't believe how stupid we've been. We were so busy tiptoeing around one another that we couldn't see the wood for the trees, if you'll excuse all those mixed metaphors.'

She laughed. 'I'll let you off just this once.'

'So long as I don't mix up my metaphors or my words ever again.' He pulled her to him and smiled into her eyes. 'I shall be very clear from now on so watch my lips, Dr Daniels. I love you and I refuse to let you leave me or Summerfield. Even if it causes umpteen problems we will solve them together. So now there's no reason why we can't get married, is there?'

'Married?' She stared at him in shock. '*Married*?'

'If you'll have me, of course, which I hope you will.' He dropped to his knees, his eyes full of love and laughter as he stared up at her. 'Maybe it's this room but I feel the need to do this properly, so… Helen Daniels, will you do me the honour of agreeing to become my wife?'

Helen giggled, then she laughed, and then she sobbed. 'Yes…oh, yes, yes!'

'That's all I needed to hear.' He stood up and swept her into his arms. She gasped as he carried her out of the room and along the hall.

'Where are you taking me?'

'Home. To my house.' He dropped a kiss on her lips then set her on her feet. 'From this point on that is where you'll be living. With me and Kristy. And I'm sure that she will grow to love you as much as I do. We are going to be a proper family—you, me, Kristy and our baby.'

Tears sparkled in her eyes as she reached up and kissed him. 'I can't think of anything I want more than to spend my life with you.'

'Me neither,' he whispered as he kissed her back. 'Me neither.'

He drew back and she could see the joy in his face. 'I'll just fetch Kristy then we can go home and start our new life together.'

MILLS & BOON®    0306/03b

Live the emotion

_Medical
romance™

HER BOSS AND PROTECTOR *by Joanna Neil*

Dr Jade Holbrook's first day in A&E doesn't go
as planned. She discovers her landlord, Callum
Beresford, is also her new boss! Jade knows she
hasn't made a good impression on the handsome
consultant, and is aware that he is watching her
every move...

*A&E DRAMA: Pulses are racing in these
fast-paced dramatic stories*

THE SURGEON'S CONVENIENT FIANCÉE
by Rebecca Lang

Theatre Nurse Deirdre Warwick is determined that
the two children left in her care will have the best
life possible. When Dr Shay Melburne enters her
life suddenly, Deirdre finds herself falling hopelessly
in love with him – and then he offers her a marriage
of convenience...but can he offer her his love?

THE SURGEON'S MARRIAGE RESCUE
by Leah Martyn

Adam Westerman is a successful Sydney surgeon and
has returned to the Outback to find the beautiful
ex-wife he's never managed to forget. Charge
nurse Liv Westerman fears Adam has only come for
custody of their child. She finds herself hoping that
he has come back for both of them...!

On sale 7th April 2006

*Available at WHSmith, Tesco, ASDA, Borders, Eason,
Sainsbury's and most bookshops*

www.millsandboon.co.uk

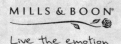

FREE!

4 Books

and a surprise gift!

We would like to take this opportunity to thank you for reading this Mills & Boon® book by offering you the chance to take FOUR more specially selected titles from the Medical Romance™ series absolutely FREE! We're also making this offer to introduce you to the benefits of the Reader Service™—

* ★ FREE home delivery
* ★ FREE gifts and competitions
* ★ FREE monthly Newsletter
* ★ Exclusive Reader Service offers
* ★ Books available before they're in the shops

Accepting these FREE books and gift places you under no obligation to buy, you may cancel at any time, even after receiving your free shipment. Simply complete your details below and return the entire page to the address below. You don't even need a stamp!

YES! Please send me 4 free Medical Romance books and a surprise gift. I understand that unless you hear from me, I will receive 6 superb new titles every month for just £2.80 each, postage and packing free. I am under no obligation to purchase any books and may cancel my subscription at any time. The free books and gift will be mine to keep in any case.

M6ZEF

Ms/Mrs/Miss/Mr ....Initials........................
BLOCK CAPITALS PLEASE

Surname ....

Address ....

....

....Postcode........................

Send this whole page to:
UK: FREEPOST CN81, Croydon, CR9 3WZ